COMPLETELY CAPTIVATED

Heartfelt Love Stories About Real Couples

by

CRYSTAL JOY

Edited by: Daisycakes Creative Services
Cover design by: VamosWrite.com
Interior Design and Formatting by: BB eBooks

Print Edition
ISBN: 978-1537777283

The idea for this book began years ago at a festival when I met a writer who wrote poems for people. As festivalgoers walked by his stand, he would ask if they wanted a poem, but not just any poem—a poem written just for them. After having a brief conversation and getting to know the people, he would write a poem, and then give it to them as a keepsake. I thought it was a fantastic idea! What a great way to connect with readers by creating something special for them.

Keeping that idea in mind, I started writing true love stories for couples and posting them on my website. In the last year, I've met many wonderful people with such captivating stories, and I wanted to give them more than just a published story on my website. I wanted to give them something they could put on their bookshelves and read to their children and grandchildren.

I am thrilled to have this first collection in print and e-book, so that friends, family, and romance readers can enjoy these special memories forever. I hope these love stories touch your heart as much as they did mine.

To read more about each couple, click on the Extras page at www.crystaljoybooks.com.

For my family.
Without you, my dream would just be
a whisper in the wind.

Acknowledgments

The acknowledgments page is one of my favorite pages to read in a book. It holds a lot of significance, especially for a new author. I've imagined writing this page since I was a little girl with a big dream to publish books. Now, it's not a dream anymore. It's a reality, and I have so many wonderful people to thank for supporting me on this journey.

So thank you a million times over …

First, to Mike, my husband. Without your support, I'd still be writing novels at five o'clock in the morning before going to work full-time. Thank you for putting up with me when I go into "writer-mode," ignoring the real world around me and thank you for reading my sappy stories, even though you'd rather read something more practical, like how to fix the kitchen sink … and yes, that's a hint. I think I clogged the drain again.

To my children. If I had to choose people to distract me from writing, I'm so glad it's you two, my little cuddle bugs. I am forever blessed to be your mom.

To Mom and Dad, my cheerleaders. You've believed in me from the very beginning. You saw something in my writing, even when it was words scribbled in a notebook. Without your encouragement, I never would've taken the plunge to pursue a writing career. I couldn't ask for better parents.

To all four of L.J. and Z.E.'s grandparents for hanging out with them, so Mama can have more time to work. I love watching their little eyes light up whenever they see you.

To Janice, my amazing critique partner. Thank you for reading my books from first to last draft. I cannot imagine working with any other business partner.

To Lisa Kimbrough-Rodriguez for all of your talented work creating my business cards, invites, and bookmarks. I'm so glad I have an excuse to connect with my sister more often.

To the Fab Five (Mandie Leytem, Jenny Lauritsen, Lyra VanLanduyt, and Sarah Larsen). A girl couldn't ask for a better group of friends.

To all of my supportive family and friends for your on-going encouragement, especially Jen Tucker, Heidi Kalafut, Carly Errico, Kathy Cline, Ben

Hoffman, and Nicole Thomason. Your confidence in me means more than you will ever know.

To the Quad City Scribblers for our monthly discussions about writing craft, publishing, and so much more. Your individual passions continue to inspire me.

To all the couples who submitted love stories. Without you, this book would not be possible. You shared the intimate details of your relationships and I am grateful for the opportunity to connect with all of you.

To my church family and Bible study ladies, for keeping me sane. Seriously.

To Sharon Hatten, for buying me my first book about publishing.

And last, but definitely not least, God. Thank you for bringing all these amazing people into my life.

TABLE OF CONTENTS

RACE TO THE ALTAR

STANDING IN THE MIDDLE of the crowded parking lot, Lisa Kimbrough bent over, sticking her butt in the air. She dug her sneakers into the pavement and leaned to the left, then to the right, as she stretched her calves one at a time. Short blond curls dangled in front of her glasses. Straightening, she pushed the strands aside with the back of her hand, only to have them fall in front of her face again.

Sighing, she dropped her hand and gave up. She had more pressing matters to worry about than her unruly hair. Like the weather. This morning the forecaster had predicted rain. And not just the typical, once-a-day Florida sprinkle, but a heavy, torrential downpour. Normally, it wouldn't be such a big deal. A rainy day meant cuddling on the couch with Joe, sending flirtatious text messages to each other as if they were far apart. But today wasn't a day for cuddling. Today they were getting married.

Outside.

A rumble of thunder reverberated across Red Bug Lake Park. She glanced up at the darkening sky, biting her bottom lip. Gray, puffy clouds loomed overhead and light sprinkles plopped into the nearby lake. Ripples spread across the still, murky water. A light wind picked up, weaving through the thick pine trees along the bike path. Cold raindrops landed on her arm.

She shivered. Rain, rain, go away, come again another day. Seriously. After all the planning and creating—the RSVP registration forms, the racer bib invites, the personalized racer T-shirts—their one mile fun run/wedding couldn't happen in the rain.

She brought a hand to her lips, biting her fingernails as Joe pressed through the crowd and jogged over, dressed in black shorts and a white T-shirt with their Race to the Altar logo. Even though she'd already seen him, her breath caught in her throat, and for a moment, she forgot about the weather. His athletic shorts fit snugly on his slim hips and stopped just below his knees, showing off his lean, muscular calves. The T-shirt clung to his hard, flat stomach and the white cotton made his complexion appear creamy and bronzed, like the color of Mario

Lopez's skin.

Her knees went weak as he stopped in front of her and wrapped his arms around her waist. His dark brown eyes filled with concern. "Something's wrong if you're biting your fingernails." He gently pulled her hand away from her mouth and kissed the inside of her palm. "You aren't having second thoughts, are you?"

"Of course not." Keeping her gaze locked on her fiancé, she pointed at the sky. A raindrop landed on her fingertip and slid down to her palm. "I'm worried about the weather."

"I'm sure the rain will let up soon."

She bit the inside of her cheek. "What if it doesn't?"

"Don't worry about the things you can't control." Closing his eyes, he leaned in close and pressed his lips against her forehead.

His soft, gentle touch sent heat pooling into her chest, traveling through her stomach, down to her toes. No matter how many times Joe kissed her, she had the same visceral reaction, as if she was standing in front of a warm heater.

Joe took a step back, his lips leaving her forehead, and she opened her eyes to see his face still inches away from hers. He lifted his chin, determination flashing in his eyes. "Even if it starts pouring and it's just us and Carrie at the finish line, we will get married today."

A grin stretched across her face. Joe was right. They wouldn't let the weather stop them from getting married. But she'd have to convince her friend, Carrie, to stick around long enough to officiate the ceremony and make their marriage official.

Joe tucked a strand of hair behind her ear, his gaze softening. "I've been looking for someone like you for a long time. I'm not waiting any longer."

The depth of his words sent a light, airy sensation fluttering through her stomach. Throughout his thirties, Joe had been in serious relationships, but he'd never found anyone he wanted to marry, until he'd met her.

"I like your attitude, Mr. Rodriguez. I don't want to wait, either." A few years ago, she'd almost given up on finding the one. After a messy divorce, she couldn't date just anyone—for her own sake, and for Alex and Kayla's. Her kids had already experienced enough hardships and she wouldn't put them through the emotional turmoil of seeing another man walk out on them. She had to find someone dependable, someone loving, someone who would stick by her side no matter what.

Thankfully, she'd met Joe on OKCupid.com. They'd made an instant connection and from the very beginning, she knew he was someone worthy of her children.

"You guys make me sick," said a familiar voice above the noisy chatter.

Lisa tore her gaze away from Joe to see her sister maneuvering through the crowd. By now, the parking lot was completely full of friends and family, wearing the same white T-shirts and a variety of brightly colored tutu's, athletic shorts, and tennis shoes.

Nicole's dark red hair bounced across her shoulders as she made her way toward them, carrying a sparkling tiara with a short, white veil attached to it. "I know you're in love and all that, but someone has to make sure the race starts on time." She grinned at Lisa. "So I guess that would be me."

Lisa glanced down at her watch. "Holy crap. The race starts in ten minutes."

"Yeah, so you need to put this on." Nicole held up the tiara, straightening out the veil.

"Will you do it?"

"Of course. Come here."

Lisa stepped forward and bent her neck, bringing her chin to her chest. The tiara dug into her scalp, followed by light tugging as Nicole positioned the bottom of the veil across her shoulders. She caught a whiff of her sister's lavender perfume. Closing her eyes, she inhaled the scent and felt a tight squeeze in her chest. If only her sister lived closer. A few years ago, Nicole had decided to be a traveling nurse before taking a permanent position at a hospital in Alaska—a.k.a way too far from Florida. If that wasn't bad enough, her younger brother and sister lived in the Midwest, and neither one could travel to Florida this weekend. Even though she understood, she couldn't help feeling a twinge of disappointment. It would've been nice to have all four of them together.

"Okay, I'm done."

Lisa opened her eyes and looked up, glancing from Nicole to Joe. "How do I look?"

Behind his glasses, Joe's eyes glistened. He blinked away the moisture and a grin stretched across his clean-shaven face. "You look beautiful."

Lisa giggled at his emotional reaction. "Aw,

you're so sweet." She leaned in close to kiss him when Nicole cleared her throat, no doubt reminding them to hurry. Lisa gave Joe a quick peck on the cheek. "Are you ready?"

He reached for her hand, squeezing it. "To marry you? I've never been more ready for anything in my entire life."

Her chest constricted. "I feel the same way."

LISA FOLLOWED JOE THE SHORT DISTANCE between the parking lot and the bike path. He stopped above the start line and turned to face their friends and family. As he turned, the sun peeked through the puffy clouds, sending bright rays across his face. Lisa clapped her hands in childlike delight. Within the last ten minutes, the rain had stopped and the black sky was turning gray. Hopefully, the weather would hold up until the race and ceremony were over.

Joe stuck two fingers in his mouth, blowing out a long, shrill whistle. The crowd went silent.

"I'd like to say a prayer before we get started."

Lisa bowed her head, Joe's words drowned out by the sound of her pounding heart. She was suddenly nervous. Not to marry Joe; the ceremony would come after the race. Her nerves had more to do with the race itself. Hopefully, everyone would stay safe and have fun. Some people weren't thrilled to exercise, but it was the perfect way to start their wedding. When she and Joe had met, they were both overweight. Toward the beginning of their relationship, they had spent most of their dates running races together, in an attempt to lose weight.

Joe concluded the prayer and walked toward Lisa, stopping next to her as Patricia stepped over the start line to sing the National Anthem. "What so proudly we haile'd …"

As Patricia sang, little arms wrapped around Lisa's waist, just above her white tutu. "Mom, can I run with you?"

Lisa glanced down at Kayla and ran a hand through her daughter's long brown hair. "You're going to run with Grandpa, okay?"

Kayla nodded and Joe scooped her up, tickling her ribs. Kayla gave a toothless smile, then let out a cute giggle. Lisa's heart swelled. Joe would be such a good father. He loved Kayla and Alex like they were his own.

As Patricia sang the last note of the National

Anthem, Joe set Kayla down on the pavement, and Mom walked in front of the crowd, holding an air horn. Her loud, confident voice carried across the parking lot. "Runners, take your positions."

Beside her, Joe rubbed his palms together and bounced from foot to foot. Leaning sideways, he nudged her shoulder. "I'll see you at the finish line, Bite Sized Boo."

"Bring it." Lisa smiled at her nickname and set one leg in front of her, bent at the knee. Adrenaline shot through her veins. This was it. The moment she'd been waiting for since they came up with the idea to have a race-themed wedding.

Mom lifted the air horn into the air. "Ready … set … go!"

Joe shot off down the trail. His lean, muscular calves propelled him down the path. His arms pumped faster as he darted ahead of the pack. He'd probably be the first to finish the race.

Her heart filled with pride. One hundred pounds ago, Joe would've been at the back of the crowd, gasping for air. And she would've been right beside him—sixty-five pounds heavier. Together, they were truly better people—physically and emotionally.

As Joe rounded the first corner, he took a quick glance back, scanning the runners. It didn't take long for him to find her. Winking, he blew her a kiss and turned his attention back to the path in front of him.

Laughter bubbled in her chest as she pushed forward, the familiar burn igniting in her calves. Fueled with Joe's encouragement, she picked up speed. The faster she ran, the sooner she'd see him at the finish line. She couldn't imagine a better prize.

LISA CLUTCHED HER PURPLE, BLUE, and pink bouquet in front of her chest, her heart beating wildly. Partly because she'd sprinted the entire mile, and partly because the ceremony was about to begin.

Setting her tennis shoes on both sides of the finish line, she expelled a nervous breath and met Joe's gaze. He gave her a reassuring smile, followed by a knowing look—one that said, *There's nothing to be nervous about. We're just two people getting married because we're perfect for each other.*

She twisted the bouquet in her sweaty hands. It still amazed her how well they could read one another without saying a word. Sometimes it felt like they were connected, as if a wire was strung between them, sending messages from her brain to his.

Tossing her long dark hair behind her back, Carrie set the Bible under her arm and looked from Lisa to Joe. "Should I start the ceremony?"

"Yes!" Kayla squealed. She jumped up and down beside Lisa, thrusting a sneaker in the air. As she jumped, the wedding rings slid back and forth across the tightly knotted shoestrings, making a light jingling noise.

Carrie chuckled. "Well, your cute little ring bearer wants to get started."

Joe leaned forward and ruffled Kayla's hair. "Don't lose our rings, kiddo." Straightening, he adjusted his first place medal and set it above the purple Run to the Altar logo on his shirt, then glanced at Carrie. "Go ahead."

Nodding, Carrie pulled her shoulders back and lifted her chin as she looked out at the crowd, now seated in rows of folding chairs sandwiched between the bike path and the lake. "Racers! It is with great joy that we gather together to witness two participants, Joe and Lisa, as they become one in marriage."

Lisa followed Carrie's gaze and scanned the front row of familiar faces—Alex stood next to Nicole, his arm draped around his Aunt Kiki's shoulders. Mom and Dad stood on opposite sides of the duo, both staring in her direction with glistening eyes. Lisa winked at them. It meant so much to have them here, getting along for her sake.

Carrie pulled the Bible out from under her arm and opened it, flipping to a book-marked page. Her loud, confident voice carried across the grassy area. "Hebrews 12:1-3 says: 'Therefore, since we are surrounded by such a great cloud of witnesses, let us throw off everything that hinders and the sin that so easily entangles. And let us run with perseverance the race marked out for us, fixing our eyes on Jesus, the pioneer and perfecter of faith." Pausing, she lifted a piece of paper from the Bible and held it out for Joe.

Taking it, he unfolded the paper with sure, steady hands. "Lisa, today I choose you to be my lifetime running partner. To massage, roll and apply bio-freeze when needed."

Lisa giggled, remembering how much fun they'd had writing their vows. They had sat at the kitchen table, drinking strong coffee as they stayed up late, writing and rewriting line after line until they both agreed on each word.

Joe glanced up from the paper, meeting Lisa's gaze. "I promise to laugh with you when times are good, and to suffer with you when they are bad. I promise to run by your side, be the bounce in your step and hold your hand as we run to the last finish line we will cross."

Expelling another shaky breath, she took the paper from Joe and folded it in half as she repeated their vows. She'd practiced them over and over so she could look at Joe while she made the most important commitment of her life.

When she was done, Lisa gave the paper back to Carrie, who placed the vows in her Bible and set the book on the pavement.

Standing, Carrie glanced down at Kayla, keeping her voice loud enough for everyone to hear. "May I have the rings?"

Kayla nodded fervently and tossed the tennis shoe in Carrie's open hand.

Holding onto the sole, Carrie held up the shoe, showcasing it like Vanna White. "These rings are an unbroken circle, having no beginning or end, representing the enduring and unending love you have for each other. Bless, O Lord, these rings to be a sign of the vows by which this man and this woman have bound themselves to each other; through Jesus Christ our Lord. Amen."

Lowering the shoe, Carrie untied the laces. Lisa's ring slipped off the lace, dropping onto the pavement. Carrie's cheeks turned crimson. "Whoops!" She crouched down and grabbed the ring, clutching it between her fingers as she handed it to Joe.

"Way to go," he whispered with a grin. Glancing back at Lisa, he slowly slid the ring over her finger. His gentle touch sent tingles running up and down her arms. "Lisa, love has put wings on our running shoes and our race begins today. No matter where the course may carry me, I will run by your side as your husband. Take this ring as a sign of my love."

Her heart pounded as she gazed into Joe's dark brown eyes and slipped the ring on his finger. As she repeated the message, the sincerity of Joe's tone resonated within her, bringing moisture to her eyes. She had no doubt he meant what he said. Joe didn't make commitments he couldn't keep. He would stand by her side—through the ups and downs of weight loss, parenting Alex and Kayla, making career changes, growing old together through it all.

Carrie held her arms out wide. "Having thus pledged yourself to the other, I do now, by virtue of the authority vested in me by the state of Florida, pronounce you husband and wife." Her eyes lit with anticipation. "You may kiss."

The finality of the words brought a flood of emotions pouring through Lisa's body. Her lungs constricted and she could barely breathe. Joe was hers. Forever.

Unable to contain her excitement, she lunged at Joe, flinging her arms around his neck and wrapping her legs around his waist.

In one swift movement, he set his hands beneath her legs, holding her up as he tilted his head forward and brought his lips to hers. Heat burned in her chest, blazing all the way down to her toes. She curled her fingers around the back of his neck, letting her lips say it all—she couldn't wait to start her life with him.

Never, Ever

Leaning forward, Betsy Kimble flipped the kill switch and turned the keys in the ignition. The 1978 Harley-Davidson remained silent. Expelling a frustrated breath, her shoulders lowered. "What am I doing wrong?"

Sitting behind her, Fritz set his hands on her thighs. The warmth of his palms pressed into her jeans. "Remember, you need to push the start button. Use your thumb. It's right below the kill switch."

"Oh yeah, that's right." She pressed the button and held it in for a moment. The engine rumbled to life, fueling her excitement. Keeping her hands on the grips, she glanced at the rearview mirror, catching sight of Fritz.

His brown curls jutted out beneath his black helmet, stopping just below his shoulders, where a gray cut-off shirt exposed his bulging biceps. All those shifts installing tires at Firestone had really sculpted his already muscular arms. She couldn't resist touching his biceps, especially when he was driving the Harley. But today she'd have to do without. Today she got to take all the risks. Just as long as she didn't crash Fritz's bike or get pulled over, since she didn't have a motorcycle license. "I can't believe I'm doing this."

"Me either." Fritz cracked a smile, his dark blue eyes gleaming behind his lightly tinted Aviators. "Let me show you how to shift again." He spent the next few minutes reminding her how to drive the bike smoothly, his voice carrying over the loud rumble of the engine.

"I think I got it." Betsy twisted around, her pulse racing as she gazed at the road. She was seriously going to drive Fritz's motorcycle all the way from Des Moines to Carroll, Iowa, almost a hundred miles. Laughter bubbled in her chest. Mom would be shocked when they pulled into the driveway and she was the one driving instead of Fritz. No doubt Mom would think she was being reckless, and maybe she was by driving the bike on the highway. But who knew recklessness could feel so much like freedom?

Fritz wrapped his arms around her waist and she tossed her thoughts aside. Life was too short to worry. "Are you ready?" he asked.

"Ready as I'll ever be."

"You aren't scared, are you?"

She shook her head and twisted the throttle, revving the engine just to prove it.

"You're turning into a daredevil." Fritz chuckled. "It's kinda hot."

"What can I say? You bring it out in me." She engaged the clutch, twisted the throttle, and lifted her feet off the ground as the bike crawled forward. Her chest rose and fell as adrenaline pumped through her veins. *Holy crap.* She was actually driving the motorcycle to Carroll. A big smile spread across her face.

She shifted gears, just like Fritz had taught her and the motorcycle picked up speed. She drove through Des Moines and made her way toward the highway. Her heart pounded in her chest as she made a turn, and a brisk fall wind blew into her helmet.

Fritz leaned in close. "You're doing great," he said over the loud roar of the engine.

Betsy grinned. Maybe she would drive his motorcycle more often.

Seeing their entrance ramp, she shifted gears and directed the bike onto the highway. Since moving to Des Moines eight years ago, she'd driven on this road almost every weekend to visit her parents and siblings. She knew every mile marker by heart, knew which gas stations sold the best cappuccinos, which farms grew corn and which ones grew beans.

And yet, this drive was a completely different experience on a motorcycle. Without the confines of a car, she could see birds flying overhead. As she drove past a field, the smell of honeysuckle drifted across the land. She hadn't smelled honeysuckle since she was a little girl, living on the farm.

With every passing minute, her shoulders loosened. They were rushing in and around all things at once: the birds, the trees, the air. Like nature was blowing her kisses.

"Look," Fritz shouted as he pointed to a tall, aluminum-sided building with two small planes parked next to it. "Remember?"

Betsy nodded. Fritz had gone skydiving there. She would never forget that day. She had stood in the open field, admiring Fritz from the ground as he jumped from the plane, soaring through the clear blue sky. He wasn't scared of anything. Within minutes, his parachute shot into the air and he descended toward the ground. Her heart hammered in her chest as she waited for him to land safely. When he did, she had jumped into his arms, wrapped her legs around his waist, and kissed him. That was the day she knew she was in love.

"You should do it with me sometime."

With the wind whipping by, she could barely make out his words. No way had he just asked her to skydive with him. She must have misheard. "Skydive?"

"Yeah," he shouted. "It's such a rush. You'd love it."

She shook her head. Just thinking about it made her stomach somersault. So many things could go wrong. She could jump at the wrong time. She could forget how to pull the parachute and spiral through the air before crashing to her death. She could jump wrong and get tangled in the strings. She could land wrong and break her legs.

"Pull over," he said loud and clear.

"Right now?"

"Yeah."

Betsy spotted a familiar red and green Sinclair

sign up ahead. Shifting gears, she pulled off the highway and headed toward a parking spot in front of the gas station.

As the motorcycle slowed to a stop, she lowered her legs and kicked the metal stand down on the pavement.

Sliding off the seat, Fritz reached for her hand and helped her off the bike.

She scrunched her nose. "Why'd we stop?"

Fritz unclasped the strap below her neck and gently lifted the helmet off her head, then hung it on the mirror. Static clung to her hair and she quickly ran a hand through her long, brown locks.

He reached for her hand again and set it above his open palm. "You're thinking about everything that could go wrong, aren't you?"

"Maybe."

"Don't."

Betsy swallowed hard. *Easier said than done.* "I would never skydive. That's just one thing you'll have to do without me."

He laughed, lighthearted and unrestrained. "You said you'd never drive my motorcycle and you're the one who wanted to drive it."

She rolled her eyes. Dang it. He had her there.

"And driving a motorcycle is a lot more dangerous than skydiving."

"That's probably true, but ..."

His thumb ran over her sparkling engagement ring, the reflection of light radiating off of his dark blue eyes. "I hate when you say you'd *never* try something. It makes me think you don't trust me." Looking up from the ring, his gaze met hers and her chest constricted. She didn't want to make him feel bad.

He put his hands on her waist and leaned in close, his cinnamon-gum breath trailing down her neck. "I would never let anything bad happen to you."

She smiled. "I know."

"Think about how much fun we would have skydiving. Just imagine me holding you close as we soar through the open sky, looking down at the amazing view beneath us."

She bit her lip, her resolve crumbling. Why did he have to be so dang convincing? Lifting her arms, she cupped Fritz's face, his five o'clock shadow feeling rough and masculine beneath her hands. "I'll go skydiving with you under one condition."

"Oh yeah? What is it?"

"Let's have the wedding in your parents' backyard. It's such a beautiful acreage and I think it would be the perfect setting."

"Deal." Fritz leaned down and gently pressed his lips to hers. Pulling her against him, he parted her lips with his, the kiss becoming deeper and more passionate.

As she kissed him back, warmth spread from her lips to her core. Her stomach did somersaults again, but this time it had more to do with Fritz's lips than the risks of skydiving. Somehow, he always had a way of making the craziest ideas sound fun and exciting. After dating for two years, she should be used to it by now. And this probably wasn't the last time he'd convince her to do something she said she wouldn't do.

BETSY RAN HER FINGER ACROSS the crease of a handmade wedding invitation and set it on the kitchen table in front of Fritz's mom.

Picking up the invitation, Mildred pressed the hole-puncher into the top corner. She poked a teal ribbon through the hole and tied a small bow, then set the invitation above the pile in the middle of the table. Leaning back in her chair, she massaged her wrinkled hands and glanced at Betsy. "Almost done."

"They look great."

"Is there anything else on your to-do list you need help with?"

"Not right now. After we get responses back from the invites, I'll have a better idea of how many centerpieces we need, then we can start working on those."

"Yes!" Fritz's voice carried from the basement, where he and his dad were watching the Packers play the Bears.

Mildred rolled her eyes. "Men and their football. I just don't get it."

Betsy shrugged. She didn't want to tell Mildred that she *did* get it. If she weren't making wedding invitations, she'd be down there watching the game with them. But the invitations needed to be sent soon. The wedding was three months away.

Mildred picked up the scissors, cutting several strands of teal ribbon. The delicate material drifted to the wooden table. Her gaze flitted from the ribbon to the pile of invitations, a faraway look in her eyes.

Betsy wiped her hands against her jeans. Did it bother Mildred that she hadn't responded? Maybe she should have agreed, after all. She wanted to have a good relationship with her future mother-in-law. Especially considering how close Fritz was with his mom and sisters. It was important for her to get along with all of them. Thankfully, she got along really well with his sisters. From the moment she'd met them, they'd treated her like family, inviting her to BBQ's, movies, and camping trips.

Mildred cut another long strand of ribbon into smaller pieces.

Clearing her throat, Betsy waited for Mildred to look up before she spoke. "Thanks for helping me today. This would've taken a lot longer without you."

"You're so sweet. You don't need to thank me." Mildred set the scissors down, a painful expression crossing her downturned face. "In fact, sometimes I think you're too sweet for my son."

Betsy narrowed her eyes. "Excuse me?"

Mildred got up from the table and waddled across the small kitchen, shutting the door to the basement.

Betsy's heart pounded. This must be serious if Mildred didn't want Fritz to hear what she had to say.

The older woman remained standing and pressed her hip against the counter. "Look, I love my son, but how do I say this?" She looked up as if the answer were written on the white popcorn ceiling. "You and Fritz just have … different interests."

Different interests? What was Mildred talking about? Sure, she and Fritz were different, but they had a lot in common, too. They were family oriented, loved to travel, and enjoyed being outdoors. And more importantly, they made each other better people. She made him more practical. And he made her more outgoing. Surely, Mildred could see that.

Her bottom lip quivered. Unless Mildred didn't like her as much as she thought. Maybe his mom was trying to break them up. But why? Mildred had to know how much they loved each other. And love was all they needed.

Betsy opened her mouth to ask.

The basement door swung open, and Fritz stepped into the kitchen, wearing ripped jeans and a black cut-off T-shirt. The silence in the room was deafening. He looked from her to Mildred, his eyebrows furrowing. "Everything okay?"

Swallowing hard, Betsy nodded. She didn't want him to know about Mildred's concerns. Not until she had answers first.

Fritz ran a hand over his jaw. He obviously knew something was wrong, but he didn't press the issue. Instead, he walked across the kitchen and grabbed his leather jacket. "John just called and invited us over. Ellen's already there. Want to go?"

"Isn't the game still on?"

"It's halftime. We can see the rest of it at John's house."

Betsy tucked a strand of hair behind her ear. She didn't want to leave without talking to Mildred, but she couldn't tell Fritz that. "Okay, let's go." She stood, the chair sliding against the faded linoleum. She scooped up the invitations, setting them inside her big, cluttered purse before glancing over at Mildred. "Thanks again for your help."

The woman's cheeks turned bright red. "You're welcome." The words came out slow and sticky like she had candy stuck to the roof of her mouth.

Outside, Betsy slid into the driver's seat of her

convertible as Fritz closed the passenger door. He turned to face her, frowning. "Tell me what happened between you and my mom."

"I don't know." Turning the keys in the ignition, she put her hand on the gearshift, reversing out of the driveway, and driving toward John's house.

Out of her peripheral vision, she could see Fritz still looking at her.

"Come on. You have no idea?"

Betsy chewed on the inside of her cheek. "She said we have different interests, and she thinks I'm too sweet for you."

"Oh, that's it? She's told me that before." Fritz laughed. "And she's right. You are too sweet for me."

She quickly glanced in his direction, narrowing her eyes. "Why would you say that?"

"You know how I am, I'm a straight shooter. I say it how it is." Fritz set his hand on the back of her seat. "But you ... Well, you're the nicest person I know. Sometimes, I think I should be more like you."

"So there's nothing I should be worried about? No other women or crazy habits I should know about?"

Fritz shook his head. "I'd be stupid to cheat on you. You're the best thing that's ever happened to me."

Heat warmed Betsy's cheeks. She wanted to believe Fritz, but she couldn't shake away the feeling that Mildred had been trying to say something else.

Twenty minutes later, they arrived at John's house. The hinges squeaked as Fritz opened the front door and she stepped inside the living room. John sat on one end of the couch, wearing sweat-pants and a loose shirt. A bag of Doritos sat between his legs, leaning against his protruding belly. On the other end of the couch, Ellen rested a hand above the armrest, carefully painting her manicured fingernails. She looked up from her pink nails, a smile spreading across her face. "Hey guys."

John stuffed a handful of Doritos in his mouth. "Good timing. The second half just started."

Ellen shot him a dirty look. "Will you please chew your food before you speak? It's totally gross when you talk with your mouth full."

"Yeah, come on, man. Don't be gross." Cracking a smile, Fritz took off his jacket and draped it across the faded blue recliner. He walked to the couch and sat down next to John. Looking up at

Betsy, he patted the open spot beside him.

She squeezed in between him and Ellen and propped her legs above Fritz's lap. He reached for one of her feet, gently rubbing his thumb into the arch. She wiggled her toes. "That feels good."

John snorted. "You two make me sick."

"That's just because you're jealous." Ellen twisted the cap back on her nail polish and brought her hands close to her mouth, blowing on the wet paint.

Betsy smiled at the easy banter. Coming over here was exactly what she needed after her conversation with Mildred. John and Ellen knew them better than a lot of people. She could just be herself and not worry if there was something she was missing.

A low growl gurgled in Ellen's stomach.

Betsy laughed. "Hungry?"

Ellen nodded, her blond bob bouncing up and down. "We ordered a pizza earlier and it's taking forever to get here." Her stomach growled again. "Ugh, I'm starving. I could eat my arm at this point."

Betsy shook her head. "You're so dramatic."

A commercial for the new F-150 played on the TV. John dropped his bag of Doritos on the shag carpet and glanced at Fritz. "Dude, I have to show you the new sound system I just put in my truck."

"Sweet. Let's go." Fritz leaned over and kissed Betsy's cheek. "Don't miss me too much."

She rolled her eyes and gave him a playful push off the couch. "I'll try not to."

Fritz sent her a grin and followed John out of the living room. The back door opened as the boys headed out to John's garage.

As soon as the door clicked shut, Ellen sat up straight, her eyes gleaming with excitement. "Guess what?"

"What?"

"I met someone."

"Who?" Betsy twisted toward Ellen, crossing her legs. "Is it someone I know?"

"Have you met Collin? The new guy at Firestone?"

"No, but Fritz told me about him. He started a couple weeks ago, right?"

"Yup. I went in to get my tires rotated, and he was working at the front desk." Ellen fanned her face. "He is *so* cute."

Betsy smiled at her friend. "I'll have to bring Fritz lunch next week so I can check this guy out."

The back door squeaked open, letting in cold

fall air. "Betsy?"

"Yeah?"

"Will you bring my jacket out here? We're gonna hang out in the garage for a while." Fritz left the door open, but his footsteps receded.

A pinch of disappointment squeezed Betsy's chest. After spending most of the afternoon making invitations, she wanted more time with Fritz. Maybe she'd ask him to come over to her apartment tonight, and she'd make him dinner. She frowned at the idea. She hated cooking. On second thought, maybe they could order from Gino's and watch *Grease*.

Pleased with her decision, she hopped off the couch and walked over to the recliner, grabbing Fritz's jacket. Draping it over her arm, she caught a whiff of his cologne, musky and woodsy—her favorite smell in the whole world. She couldn't get enough of it.

A small plastic bag dropped out of a pocket and landed on the floor. Crouching down, Betsy picked up the bag. It was filled with round white pills.

Her lips fell open. "What are these?"

"Let me see." Ellen stood and took the bag, examining the pills. "It's speed," she said matter-offactly.

"Speed? As in, the drug?" Betsy's heart hammered in her chest as she waited for an answer.

"I think so."

"You're wrong." Betsy gave a slow, disbelieving headshake. "It's probably aspirin or ibuprofen."

Ellen handed the bag back, careful not to mess up her freshly painted nails. "I doubt it. Fritz probably got the speed from John."

"What are you talking about?"

Ellen's eyebrows creased together. "I thought you knew." Her expression was sympathetic. "John's a drug dealer."

"You can't be serious." Betsy pressed a hand against her coiling stomach. The walls closed in on her, making it difficult to breathe. Ellen had to be wrong. John couldn't be a dealer. She would never be friends with a drug dealer. More importantly, she wouldn't be engaged to druggie.

She glanced at the pills again, swallowing hard as her conversation with Mildred emerged all too quickly. *You're too sweet for my son.* Because he does drugs? Was that what his mom had meant?

Ellen put her hand on Betsy's shoulder. "I'm really sorry you found out this way."

Blinking away the moisture in her eyes, she lifted her chin, meeting Ellen's gaze. "I need to talk to Fritz." With trembling hands, she clutched the bag and rushed out of the house.

Fritz had some explaining to do.

RAINDROPS DRIPPED DOWN THE WINDOWPANES as vibrant red and yellow watercolors filled the sky and the sun began its descent. Betsy twisted the blinds shut and turned to Fritz. The last month had been hard. Tonight, they needed to have some fun together. "It looks like the sky is clearing up. Do you want to go take the bike out after dinner?"

Fritz set two steaming plates of spaghetti on the coffee table and gave her a knowing look. "You just want to drive it again, don't you?"

"Maybe." She drew out the word.

"I'm gonna start calling you my motorcycle mama."

Betsy laughed, the foreign sound reverberating in her ears. She couldn't remember the last time she'd laughed with Fritz. It felt good.

He sat down on the couch and waited for her to

sit next to him before he pulled a faded Packers blanket over their laps. She leaned into him as he draped his arm across her shoulders and pressed his lips against her cheek. His soft, loose curls tickled her skin.

For a moment, he didn't move. "I love you." His warm breath glided down her neck, sending tingles down her spine.

"I love you, too." She closed her eyes, wishing their relationship could always be this easy. In the last month, it had been anything but. That day at John's, she'd confronted Fritz about the pills and he assured her they weren't speed. He said the medicine was for his acid reflex. His dad had acid reflux, too, and he'd given Fritz some of the pills from his container the day they'd visited his parents.

Fritz also reminded her how dramatic Ellen could be. He said John used to be a drug dealer, but he stopped after getting a full-time job at Firestone. Everything Fritz had said made sense.

And yet, she couldn't trust him completely. Questions pricked her heart like needles, injecting doubts that wouldn't go away. Was she making the right choice to marry him? She wanted a husband who was fun and adventurous, but she needed more than that. Was he really the hardworking, dependable, trustworthy guy she thought he was?

Brushing hair away from her face, Fritz trailed kisses down her neck. His soft lips made it hard to think and she pushed her worries away. Why waste a perfectly good night when things were going so well between them at the moment?

A shrill ring buzzed from the telephone on the end table. Sighing, Fritz stopped kissing her and leaned across the couch, reaching for the phone. The short cord stretched from the end table to the armrest. Fritz lifted the phone off its base. "Hello?"

As he listened to the caller, his mouth formed a thin line. "She's right here. Hold on a sec." He cupped his hand over the receiver and met Betsy's gaze. "It's for you. It's Ellen."

Pushing the blanket off her lap, Betsy stood and walked to the end table. She took the phone from Fritz, clutching it against her ear. "Hey. What's up?"

"Sorry to bother you. I tried calling your apartment first, but you weren't there."

"Is everything okay?"

"Well ..." The line went silent for a moment before Ellen continued. "I just thought you'd want to know that John was arrested."

Betsy's eyes widened. "For what?"

"He got pulled over for speeding and the police found all kinds of drugs in his truck. Like speed, crack, and meth."

The blood rushed out of Betsy's face.

"It's in the paper if you don't believe me."

Her heart picked up pace, hammering so hard it would surely explode. She dropped the phone and rushed into Fritz's kitchen, grabbing the paper off the kitchen table. Flipping through the flimsy pages, she stopped at the Police Blotter and brought it close to her face. She scanned the list of arrests and sure enough, John's name was on it.

"What's going on?" Fritz's voice came from behind her.

Betsy whirled around, standing a foot away from him and shoved the paper at his chest with trembling hands.

His eyebrows creased together as he scanned the page.

"John isn't a dealer anymore, huh? Then why was he caught with drugs?" She put a hand on her hip, anger and hurt pulsating through her body. "You lied to me."

Fritz let go of the paper, letting it glide to the

kitchen floor. His Adam's apple bobbed up and down as he opened his mouth, then closed it.

"You lied to me," she repeated. "That wasn't acid reflex medicine. It was speed, wasn't it? Tell. Me. The truth."

Fritz ran a hand through his curly hair, a guilt-ridden expression crossing his downturned face. "Yeah." He said the word so quietly she barely heard him.

"Does your mom know? Is that what she'd meant?"

"Yeah."

Swallowing hard, Betsy shook her head. She should have known. She'd been too naïve, too in love with him to see the truth. "How could you lie to me?"

"I didn't want to lose you." He took a step forward, breaking the space between them. "I can't imagine my life without you. I love you so much."

Betsy snorted in disgust. "You have a funny way of showing it."

"I won't do it anymore. I'll stop. I promise." Fritz reached for her hand, his gaze meeting hers. Regret flashed in his dark blue eyes.

Blinking back tears, she pulled away and took a

step back. "Don't touch me." She turned around, no longer able to look at him. Pain tore through her insides, ripping her heart to shreds. She'd given him a second chance. Because she loved him. Because she wanted to marry him.

Tears pooled in her eyes, stinging. She couldn't hold them back any longer. They streamed down her face, pouring down as steady as the rain had earlier this evening.

Marching toward the front door, she shoved her tennis shoes on and swung the door open. She dashed outside, taking the steps two at a time. She made a beeline across the yard, heading toward her car that was parked next to the curb. Her shoes sunk into the wet grass.

"Wait." Fritz followed her out the door, his voice drenched with desperation. "I'll do anything to make it up to you."

"That should have been your response the first time," she muttered, more to herself than to him. She spun on her heels, staring at the monster who had broken her heart.

He stood on the porch, his bare feet curling over the edge of the first step. His shoulders were slightly hunched over and his large, muscular arms hung at his sides. He looked like he'd just found out his childhood pet had died. "I messed up."

"That's an understatement." Betsy lifted her chin, not feeling sorry for him in the slightest.

"What else do you want me to say?"

She twisted the ring on her finger. No marriage should start out this way. She could never trust Fritz again. Fool me once, shame on you. Fool me twice, shame on me. She'd heard that saying enough to know it must be true.

Choking back a sob, she slowly slid the beautiful ring off her finger like tearing off a scab. With tear-filled eyes, she glanced at Fritz one last time. "There's nothing left to say." She hurled the ring into the grass and turned around without looking back.

Her breathing grew rapid as tears flowed down her cheeks. She could barely see as she walked toward her convertible and slumped inside. Her whole body shook. She would never trust another man with her heart again. They weren't worth it.

Better yet, she would never, ever get married. She would be just fine on her own.

Walls of Glass

Stephanie Platt stopped at the end of the serving line, scanning the crowded cafeteria at Ozark Christian College. Giggles erupted from a table of girls as a blond Barbie babbled to her friends. A group of big, burly guys shoved fries in their mouths. A few feet away, a couple held hands across their table, gazes locked above goofy grins. The guy rubbed his thumb on the top of the girl's hand as he spoke, and her cheeks turned the same color as the strawberries on her salad.

Stephanie wrinkled her nose. Why would anyone spend the first semester of college stuck in a relationship? First semester was supposed to be about having fun. Meeting lifelong friends. Learning about yourself and growing as a person. Dating would definitely distract from doing all of that.

"Stephanie." A deep, quiet voice came from behind.

She turned as Caleb walked toward her, wearing faded jeans and a black zip-up hoodie. Beneath a green army hat, his root beer colored eyes met her gaze.

She looked down at the floor, her pulse picking up speed. Had Caleb really remembered her name? Two weeks ago, she'd met him and his friends on the promenade, and she figured he'd forgotten her by now.

His loosely tied KEDS stopped beside her flip-flops. "I was hoping I'd run into you again."

Her head jerked up. "You were?"

"Yeah. We didn't have a lot of time to talk the other day. Do you want to eat together?"

She bit her lower lip. "Um, sure. My friend's sitting over there."

"Great. I'll follow you."

With shaky legs, Stephanie slipped into a seat beside Bethany and introduced her friend to Caleb as he pulled out a chair across the table. She tried to steady her breathing. What was wrong with her? She shouldn't be reacting this way. She didn't have time for some meaningless relationship that would only lead to heartbreak. Most guys didn't look for serious girlfriends so early in college and no way would she fall prey to a guy who just wanted a fling, even if he *was* cute.

Bethany tossed long dark locks behind her shoulder. "How do you know each other?"

"I met Caleb and his friends on the promenade."

"During the faith forum?"

"No, just between classes," Stephanie said.

Caleb smiled. "I'm glad you came over to talk."

"Wait." Bethany raised her eyebrows. "Steph introduced herself to you?"

"Yup," Stephanie answered before he could. As far as Caleb knew, she wasn't shy and introduced herself to guys all the time. In reality, it was the first time she'd ever done it. That day it felt like someone else had taken over her body, giving her the confidence to walk over to the group of guys and start talking to them. She immediately noticed Caleb, standing quietly in the group. Even though he hadn't said much, it was clear the others respected Caleb by the way they addressed him.

She picked up her fork and cut into the calzone, marinara oozing onto her plate. Biting into the too-cool crust, she chewed on the rubbery pepperoni and swallowed. "I miss my mom's lasagna."

Caleb nodded. "I know. My mom's cooking is

so much better."

"Where are you from?" she asked.

"Davenport, Iowa."

She dropped her fork and put a hand to her chest. "I'm from Iowa, too."

"What city?"

"Cedar Falls."

Caleb blinked, the tip of his long dark lashes gracing his cheeks. "Where's that?"

"It's by ..." Grabbing a napkin, she pointed to a spot in the upper center. "If this is Iowa, I live right here."

He gave a lighthearted laugh. "That's the best way you could tell me?"

She picked up her fork again and pointed it at him. "Hey, it's the best I could think of at the moment."

Caleb held up his hands in mock innocence. "Okay, okay. I'll let it go for now." Lowering his elbows, his hand bumped against the tray. Food tumbled onto his lap. He pushed back his chair, the uneaten calzone sliding down his jeans and plopping on the tiled floor.

"Oh no!" Stephanie pointed to the food and laughed.

Caleb bent down and picked it up, tossing it back onto his tray. As he took a napkin to his jeans, he flashed a smile, exposing white teeth that would make any dentist proud. "So much for my lunch."

Stephanie cut her calzone in half. "You can have some of mine."

"Thanks."

She carefully set it on his tray. Silence settled over the table as he took a bite.

Bethany cleared her throat. "What's your major, Caleb?"

"I want to go into the medical field as a missionary." He cautiously set his elbows on the table, his gaze focusing on Stephanie. "What about you?"

Bethany sighed and Stephanie gave her friend an apologetic smile before looking back at Caleb. "I want to be a missionary, too. But I'm starting to worry. I miss my family a lot and I've only been away from them for a couple of weeks. I'm not sure how long I'll be able to last when I'm halfway across the world in some third world country without wireless."

"I know. I have a five-year-old sister at home. It sucks being away from her."

Stephanie's heart fluttered. How sweet that

Caleb would readily admit to missing his little sister. He was definitely different from any other guy she'd met.

Not that it mattered. She had a deal with God to uphold: She wouldn't date a guy unless she was willing to marry him. And she definitely wasn't ready for dating or marriage.

CALEB LISTON STEPPED INTO SHOAL CREEK. Water rushed up to his knees and soaked the bottom of his rolled up jeans. Up ahead, waterfalls cascaded down a 163-foot wide ledge of solid chert, crashing into the jagged crags of the creek. Sunlight glimmered off the water, its bright rays reflecting off Stephanie's dark red hair as she took a cautious step into the creek. Behind her, Marcy and Austin took off their shoes, setting them in the grass.

Caleb pointed to the waterfall closest to land. "Want to head over to that one first?"

Austin nodded. "Lead the way, man."

Caleb smiled at his friend. Austin was being a good sport. Going to Grande Falls with Stephanie and Marcy wasn't what Austin had in mind when he'd decided to visit Caleb, but he'd agreed, knowing how badly Caleb wanted to hang out with Stephanie. The two had only messaged on Facebook during the last few weeks but Caleb was hooked.

Turning around, he waited for Stephanie to stop beside him, then started toward the falls. As they treaded through the knee-deep water, he studied her profile: high cheekbones, full lips, blue-green eyes, and porcelain skin. She was absolutely gorgeous.

Thankfully, she said yes to hanging out today. Not that he could consider it a date—not with Austin and Marcy along—but, it was definitely a step in the right direction.

She tucked a long strand of hair behind her ear. "So ..."

He cracked his knuckles. Shoot. She'd probably caught him looking at her and he had no idea what to say. If only his throat wasn't so dry. He swallowed repeatedly, trying to come up with something smooth. "Tell me about your family."

"Well, I have an older sister. We're really close. My mom cleans houses and my dad's a pastor."

"Really? So is mine."

She stuck her hand in the creek, her fingers creating small ripples in the water as she moved forward. "Is that why you want to go into missionary work?"

"Uh-huh. I want to help people. Both spiritually and medically."

"Did you ever consider becoming a pastor?"

"Not really. I knew I wanted to do something different. Did you?"

Stephanie shook her head. "I'm way too shy. I'll sing in front of a church, but that's about it."

"I'd like to hear you sing sometime."

She snorted. "I don't think so."

"You'll sing in front of a church, but you won't sing in front of me?"

"That's right. I'm stubborn."

He chuckled. "Besides church, what do you do in your free time?"

"I like to scrapbook and I love baking. Cookies are my favorite. During the holidays, my mom, sister, and I spend hours in the kitchen making ginger cookies and fudge."

Caleb adjusted the hat on his head, bringing the bill slightly higher on his forehead. "I hope this doesn't sound weird, but you remind me a lot of my mom."

"How so?"

"For starters, you have the same name ..." He let the sentence trail off, his throat suddenly dry again.

Stephanie gave him a reassuring smile. "What else?"

"She scrapbooks a lot. I mean, you should see all the books she has of my brother, sister, and me. And she loves to cook. She's always having church members over at our house, cooking dinner for them."

"She sounds great."

Caleb nodded. Hopefully, one day Stephanie would meet his mom. He had no doubt they'd get along.

A comfortable silence settled between them as they neared the towering falls. From behind, Austin and Marcy grew near, their voices muffled by the crashing water ahead. The farther they walked, the bigger the rocks were. Caleb stepped on one, slimy moss seeping between his toes. He took another cautious step forward, careful not to slip. He looked back at Austin and Marcy, raising his voice so they could hear him. "Watch out; it's slippery up here."

"Whoa." Beside him, Stephanie tilted backward, her hands flailing at her sides.

Turning, he reached out and grabbed her hand, helping her regain her footing. Touching her hand sent tingles up and down his arm, and for a moment, he didn't let go. Swallowing hard, he met her gaze and his heart picked up speed. Did she notice how perfectly her hand fit inside his?

Her cheeks turned crimson as she quickly pulled her hand away. "Um, thanks."

"Yeah." He reluctantly lowered his arm and took a few more steps, standing directly in front of the falls.

Mist from the waterfall sprayed onto Stephanie's face as she stopped beside him and put her hand in the waterfall, letting it glide between her fingers. Looking up at him, a big childish grin spread across her face.

Caleb's stomach flip-flopped. He really liked her. More than that, he could see a future with her. But did she have feelings for him?

He readjusted his hat, setting it higher on his forehead. There was only one way to find out. He'd have to ask her on a date. "Steph, I was wondering ..." She stared at him expectantly and he tried to conjure enough confidence to finish the sentence. *Accio confidence!* If only Harry Potter spells worked in real life. He cracked his knuckles as she continued looking at him.

"Yeah?"

"Would you—"

"This is awesome." Austin lunged into the waterfall, disappearing behind the heavy flow of bluish-green water.

Wiping water off her face, Stephanie giggled. "What were you saying?"

Caleb opened his mouth, but nothing came out. This girl was the real deal. Someone he could see himself with for a long, long time.

His shoulders lowered. If only he had the guts to ask her out.

HEART RACING, CALEB SLID THE electronic mouse over his desk. On the computer screen, the arrow hovered above the *send* button.

He moved the mouse away and rested his elbows on the desk, scanning the contents of the email again. *I'm not romantic and I probably won't change. I'm not good at listening. In case you were wondering, I hold my head crooked because I had a lot of ear infections as a kid and I favored the other side too often. When people ask, I like to mess with them and act offended.*

And just so you know, I like you a lot.

Caleb leaned back in his chair and steepled his hands under his chin. What an understatement. Since meeting Stephanie, his whole world had changed. Every Facebook conversation with her brought a smile to his face. Being a pastor's kid, she'd grown up very similarly to him. She understood what it was like to have people coming and going from her house at all hours, to spend weekends at church and a lot of weeknights, too. But it wasn't just her past; her goals for the future were also very similar. He could already imagine going on mission trips with her, spreading the gospel to people living in third world countries, bringing them hope.

There was just one big problem. She still didn't know how he felt.

He hadn't hung out with her since they'd gone to Grande Falls a couple weeks ago. It felt like torture not to see her. Like a single raindrop in the middle of a dry desert, one drop wasn't enough to quench his thirst.

Caleb stood and paced back and forth across his small dorm room. But what would Stephanie think after she read the email? Would she think less of him? Or worse, would she never want to speak to him again?

He dropped back into his chair, the sudden weight lowering the height with a gentle swoosh. Clasping the mouse, he slid it over his desk, setting the arrow on *send* again.

He let it hover for a moment and closed his eyes. *Please God, if it is your will, let her like me as much as I like her.* Opening his eyes, he expelled a deep breath and clicked the mouse. The email disappeared.

It was a chance he had to take. She deserved to know who he really was.

But maybe he should call her and explain why he'd sent the email.

Reaching for his phone, he scrolled through his contacts list, clicking on her name. He lifted the phone to his ear and several rings buzzed through the receiver.

Stephanie's soft voice greeted him, sounding like a soothing, melodic tune.

"I just sent you an email," he said.

"Oh. Do you want me to read it right now?"

"No." Caleb rubbed the back of his neck, loosening his coiled muscles. "Actually, I wanted to tell you something."

"What?"

"I uh, I really like you."

Silence settled over the line.

"Would you go on a date with me?"

"Caleb …" She drew out his name, letting the line go quiet.

With his heart hammering, he stood and crossed the room. Surely, she had to have feelings for him by now.

"Can't we just be friends?"

Caleb collapsed onto his futon and tilted his head back, looking at the ceiling. It didn't make sense. Why would God let him feel so strongly about someone who didn't even want to go on a date with him?

STEPHANIE STEPPED OUT OF THE CHAPEL and into the sunshine. Reaching in her backpack, she pulled out a pair of sunglasses and slid them over her nose.

A warm breeze rustled through the trees, scattering orange and red leaves across the plush, green grass.

She glanced down at her watch, quickening her pace. Two hours wouldn't be enough time to finish the pile of homework crammed inside her backpack.

Opening the door to the library, she headed toward the first empty table and spread her textbooks across it. Setting *Christian Life* in front of her, she leaned forward with a highlighter in hand.

She read the first sentence, then reread it. Blinking, she read it again. But the words wouldn't register. Caleb's email resurfaced instead.

She leaned back in the chair, a smile tugging at her lips. He had laid it all out there. The good, the bad, and the ugly. He wanted her to know everything about him.

Tossing the highlighter in her textbook, Stephanie massaged her temples. It wasn't supposed to happen this way. She was supposed to go to college, meet new friends, study, and enjoy her college experience. None of that included dating someone, especially someone she could date seriously. Like Caleb. In the short amount of time she'd known him, she could already tell he was marriage material. The kind of guy she could bring home to meet her family.

Her friends from home would surely think she was being naïve, dating the first guy who asked her out. She couldn't be *that girl.* The one who fell hopelessly in love during her first year of college. She needed to stay away from Caleb. He was a little too good, a little too soon. Maybe in a couple years they could reconnect and start a relationship. If he was still single.

Her chest constricted. The thought of Caleb dating someone else didn't seem right, and yet, she wasn't ready for a relationship. She would have to take a risk and hope that he would remember her.

CALEB PEERED OVER THE BUFFET COUNTER, clutching a ladle full of marinara. Stephanie stopped in front of his station, dressed in jeans and a T-shirt. Her dark red locks hung in loose curls around her shoulders. She looked above the pasta options, her blue-green eyes meeting his gaze.

His stomach flip-flopped. He'd never met a woman who could look so good in casual clothes. "Want some sauce to go with your spaghetti?"

"Yes, please."

He spread the marinara over her noodles as awkward silence settled between them.

Stephanie picked at the edge of her tray with her thumbnail. "It's been a while." One month and three days, not that she'd been counting.

"I know." He had to think of something else to say, something that would give him more time with Stephanie. He glanced up at the clock. "I get off work in a half hour. I thought I'd hit up Starbucks after that." He paused and took a breath. *Come on, don't be a wuss. Just ask her.* "Do you … Do you want to go with me?"

As he waited for a response, he set the ladle back in the marinara sauce and cracked his knuckles. If Stephanie said no, he wouldn't ask her out again. He had to respect her wishes. He would give up and move on, even though he didn't want to. Stephanie wasn't the type of woman he could easily forget.

She bit her lower lip. "Yeah. I'll go with you."

A grin spread across his face. Even if she didn't want to date him, at least he could spend time with her.

Half an hour later, Caleb and Stephanie found a table, sandwiched between a gray-haired man reading the Bible and two girls texting on their cell phones. Voices buzzed across the warm room. Mocha and caramel perfumed the air.

Caleb lifted the straw to his lips, sipping from a vanilla frappe. Beneath the table, his leg bounced to the rhythm of classical music playing softly from the speakers. "After you graduate, do you plan on moving back to Iowa?"

"Yeah. I wouldn't want to live too far away from my sister." She dipped her finger in the top layer of whip cream on her frappe and licked it off her finger. "Especially after we get married and start families of our own."

"How many kids do you want?"

"At least two."

"That's a good number." Caleb smiled. "If I ever have a daughter, I want to be one of those dads who gets out his shotgun when a guy comes to the door asking to take her out."

Stephanie laughed. "I was always afraid my dad would do that. Or worse, run outside the house with his gun as the guy pulled up in our driveway, but …"

"But what?"

She tucked a strand of hair behind her ear. "I've

never dated anyone."

"Oh." Caleb's eyes widened.

"Why do you look so surprised?"

"It doesn't take long to realize you're a catch." The words came out so quickly he barely had time to realize he'd said them out loud. Not that he regretted it. What he'd said was true.

She shifted in her chair, looking uncomfortable.

Caleb frowned. The last thing he wanted to do was make her feel uneasy. If only she would open up to him. Not wanting to press the issue yet, he glanced out the window at the fading sun. "Want to go for a drive?"

"Okay."

In the car, Caleb drove down Main Street, a long straight road between school and the nearby neighborhoods. Stephanie's lilac perfume wafted through the vehicle. His heart pounded in his chest. He took his eyes off the road, glancing in her direction. "Can I ask you a personal question?"

Stephanie laughed. "Sure."

"What are you afraid of?"

"Excuse me?"

Keeping one hand on the wheel, he rubbed a sweaty palm against his jeans. "We've spent hours talking on Facebook and when I'm with you, it seems like you like me. So why are you afraid to go out with me?"

Stephanie looked out the window as they passed by campus. "I do like you. That's the problem. I like you too much."

"You like me too much to date me?" Caleb arched his eyebrow. "That doesn't make sense."

"I know. I guess I'm just worried about what other people will think."

"Why does it matter?"

"It doesn't, not really. It's just ..." Using her thumb, Stephanie wiped the condensation dripping from her cup. "When I was in high school, I made a deal with God. I promised Him I'd never date anyone unless I was sure we would get married."

"That's awesome." Caleb glanced at Stephanie, thoroughly impressed. Her deal with God said a lot about her. Her faith was strong, and she didn't take marriage lightly. She didn't want to waste time being in a relationship that wasn't going anywhere.

Stephanie cleared her throat, continuing. "Since I've never had a boyfriend before, how can I trust you with my heart?"

Looking back at the road, Caleb clutched the

steering wheel. After hearing about her deal with God, he felt even more certain about Stephanie than he had before. He had to convince her they were perfect together. He might not have made a deal with God, but he took dating and marriage very seriously, just like she did.

He slowed the car at the end of the street, stopping beneath a dim streetlamp. Silence invaded the small space like a heavy fog.

He turned toward Stephanie, the glow of the moon highlighting the golden irises in her eyes. "You've got walls built around your heart."

Her lips parted as her chest rose and fell.

He inched closer, his knee resting against the middle console. "The walls are glass and I can see through them, but I really want you to open the door so I can come in."

A car passed by, its headlights shining into the car as Stephanie's eyes glistened. "I want that, too."

Caleb swallowed hard. He didn't want to put pressure on her, but she had to know how much he cared. "Will you be my girlfriend?"

She set her drink in the cup holder and ran a hand through her hair.

A bead of sweat trickled down his back. She was

seriously considering what he'd said, he could feel it, but would she bolt the other way again?

She shifted in her seat and bit her lip. Then, a grin spread across her face. "Yes."

Caleb reached for her hands, his shaky fingers fumbling to clasp her hands just right.

Stephanie glanced down, her forehead furrowing. "Are we shaking hands?"

"No, I'd like to pray."

"Oh. Good idea."

Chuckling, Caleb bowed his head and entwined their fingers. As he prayed, a deep certainty settled in his heart. He would ask Stephanie to be his wife someday. Hopefully, she would say yes because he couldn't imagine his life without her.

Waiting for Prince Charming

Nestling close to Kalvin, Heidi Tangren closed her heavy eyes, exhaustion crawling through her brain. After a three-hour bike ride, she could barely stay awake to watch the movie. Instead, she listened to the quiet hum of voices coming from the TV as Aladdin rode the magic carpet up to Jasmine's balcony.

Kalvin leaned forward. "You aren't falling asleep, are you?"

Her eyelids fluttered open. "Of course not. Just resting my eyes."

"Uh-huh. Sure." Light from the TV reflected off Kalvin's glasses as he gave her a knowing look. "You can't fall asleep yet. It's not like we get to do this a lot."

"I know."

He leaned back against the couch again and she looped her arm around his, setting her head on his shoulder. She wanted to close her eyes again as their breaths fell into a steady rhythm, but she kept them open. Kalvin was right. They didn't get to see each other often enough. With a full-time job, working six days a week and living an hour away, it was hard to visit for the entire weekend.

At least they wouldn't be apart much longer. After dating for a year and a half, they'd finally made the decision to move in together. It was a step in the right direction to see if they wanted to make their relationship more serious, more permanent.

Kalvin reached for the remote, turning up the volume. "Isn't this your favorite part?"

Heidi looked at the flat screen as Aladdin and Jasmine took a magic carpet ride above Agrabah. Mimicking Aladdin, she mouthed the words to "A Whole New World." As the song ended, she blinked back the moisture in her eyes, but a lone tear escaped and trickled down her cheek. She lifted her hand, quickly wiping the tear away.

Kalvin chuckled. "You're such a sap."

Smiling, she blinked again. "I can't help it." She'd always been emotional. From the time she was a little girl, crying when the prince kissed sleeping beauty and broke the spell or when Belle threw a snowball at the beast as she fell hopelessly in love. Even as an adult, the idea of Prince Charming hadn't lost its appeal. In fact, her little girl self still believed in happily-ever-after. Maybe—no, hopefully, she could have it with Kalvin.

HEIDI LIFTED THE LARGE, juicy burger off her plate and bit into it. Her stomach growled as she swallowed the first mouthwatering bite. Barbeque sauce oozed between her fingers and dripped onto her plate.

Sitting across the booth, Kalvin raised his eyebrows. "You weren't joking."

"Ya think?" Glaring at Kalvin, she took another bite and set the burger down. She reached for a napkin, dabbing it across her mouth. She hadn't eaten anything since breakfast, seven hours ago. This morning, he had assured her that the Historic Homes Tour would only last a few hours and then they could get lunch downtown.

"I'm sorry." Kalvin rubbed his hands over his khakis, then lifted his arms above the table and rolled up the sleeves of his green dress shirt, exposing tan forearms. "I didn't know the tour would last that long."

"You should've checked."

"What else do you want me to say? I already apologized." Kalvin ran a hand over his short, brown hair. He reached for his beer and lifted it to his mouth, but instead of drinking it, he put the glass back on the table and twisted it in his hands. "How was I supposed to know all those restaurants had closed?"

"You should've ..." Heidi let the sentence trail off as Kalvin slid his glass across the table in front him, back and forth from hand to hand. Why was he so fidgety? He hadn't seemed anxious during the tour. Maybe he felt uncomfortable arguing in public. That had to be it. This wasn't their first fight, but others had been in private.

"I should've what?" Waiting for an answer, Kalvin expelled a heavy breath, his broad shoulders lowering.

Heidi adjusted her glasses, setting them higher on her nose. Maybe it had nothing to do with being in public. Maybe she was being too hard on him. She had to admit he'd planned the date with good intentions, as a way for her to learn more about the

Quad Cities before she moved here in a few weeks. "I'm sorry I've been in such a bad mood. I don't want to fight anymore."

Kalvin stopped moving his drink and met her gaze. "Me either."

Heidi reached for her IPA, tipping the glass back. The cold drink slid down her throat, washing away the last remnants of annoyance. Setting her drink on the table, she rubbed her thumb against the glass, wiping away the perspiration as she smiled at Kalvin. "I really did have a good time today."

"I did, too. Those houses were awesome."

"I can't believe Charles Deere built *two* mansions. That guy was seriously talented, not to mention romantic." She selected a fry, doused it in ketchup, and plopped it into her mouth. "Do you think Deere surprised his wife after the house was finished or do you think his wife knew about the house and helped design it?"

Kalvin gave her a lopsided grin. "He probably told her about the house."

"It would be more romantic if he'd surprised her."

"Yeah, but if the guy knew what was good for him, he would've let her design the whole place."

Kalvin leaned forward, setting his elbows on the table. "That way he wouldn't have spent the next few years remodeling things she didn't like."

Rolling her eyes, she threw a fry at Kalvin. "Hey, you're the one who wanted to remodel the house."

Kalvin dodged the fry and chuckled. "I know." He took a bite of his burger and a small dot of ketchup dripped onto his lips.

She reached across the table, gently picking off the sauce with her thumbnail. "The house looks so good. I could spend all day in that kitchen."

"That's all you. I'm just making your vision come to life."

"We make a good team." Since Kalvin had moved to the Quad Cities and bought the house, he'd spent every weekend working on it. She appreciated his do-it-yourself attitude. Not only with remodeling, but with everything around the house: the electrical work, plumbing, and landscaping.

He definitely wasn't the type of engineer who only sat at a computer, planning and designing—he was good at building things with his hands too.

He bit into his half-eaten burger and tossed it back onto his plate. "Ready to go?"

She glanced at the fries still piled on his plate. "Don't you want to finish dinner?"

He shrugged. "Not really." His cheeks turned crimson as he twisted in his seat and glanced out the window beside their booth. "We should go for a walk."

Her lips parted. Why was Kalvin acting strange again? Was he still upset with her for being in a bad mood earlier? She didn't want to bring it up again, so she followed his gaze instead. The sun peeked through puffy white clouds drifting across the blue, watercolor sky. It *was* a beautiful night for a walk. If only she wasn't dressed in a lacy top, pencil skirt, and high heels.

Turning to face her, his blue eyes eagerly met hers, as if he knew she needed coaxing. "When I was on the bike trail yesterday, I found this cool park I really want you to see."

She bit her lip, contemplating a response. She didn't want to disappoint him, but she wouldn't walk on a bike path in high heels. Her feet would be torn to pieces and she liked wearing heels at work. It made her appear more professional in front of customers, especially since Hands Jewelers only sold high quality jewelry.

She tugged on her lacy shirt and looked at Kalvin, who was staring at her expectantly. “Let’s change into comfortable clothes first.”

Frowning, Kalvin scratched his chin. “Okay.”

Her eyebrows creased together. Why would he have a problem with changing their clothes? Something was definitely bothering him.

She swallowed hard. Hopefully, it wasn’t anything serious.

LIFTING LONG BLOND STRANDS OFF HER NECK, Heidi pulled her hair back into a ponytail. Even with an hour left of daylight, the sweltering humidity still hung in the air.

Beside her, Kalvin slipped his hands inside the pockets of his athletic shorts as he walked. A circle of sweat dampened his T-shirt and stuck to his chest.

Her breath caught in her throat. How could a guy look so good even when he was sweating? All those hours of training for the Quad City Half Marathon had really paid off.

She gently wrapped her fingers around his arm,

slowly moving her fingers down his forearm to reach into his pocket and grab his hand.

He pulled away as if he'd been burned.

She stopped walking, her stomach tightening. "I just wanted to hold hands."

"Oh." He lifted his hand from his pocket and reached for her, entwining their fingers. As they started walking again, red blotches appeared on his neck.

Why was Kalvin breaking out? Was he nervous? Did he have something he wanted to tell her? Ignoring the onslaught of questions ambushing her mind, Heidi looked around, taking in her surroundings. Beside the trail, a small creek trickled over a bed of rocks. A stone cliff bordered the farthest side of the creek, ascending to wooded backyards. An earthy dampness rose from the ground, its fresh scent diminishing her doubts. She was probably worrying for nothing. She turned her head, studying Kalvin's profile—his long brown eyelashes, pale blue eyes, his square jaw line. She tried not to stare, but it was hard not to.

He squeezed her hand. "What do you think?"

She smiled. "It's beautiful."

"Look over there," he whispered, pointing to the

trail ahead where large oak trees towered above the path. Sunlight beamed through the vibrant green leaves, casting light on two fawns leaping through the brush.

"I feel like we're in a movie, like *Bambi.*" Heidi let go of his hand and walked toward the nearest bench to watch the fawns.

He stood still as if he couldn't decide if he wanted to follow her.

She sat down anyway, and a bunny hopped near her feet, nibbling on a clover patch. "Aw, how cute."

Nodding, he walked over and stopped a few feet away from the bench. Turning his back to her, he slid his hands inside his shorts. She twisted her lips. Why wasn't he sitting down next to her? Did he see something else?

She leaned sideways, looking past him. In the creek, two ducks glided past. But he wasn't looking at them. He was messing with something in his pocket. She furrowed her eyebrows. Seriously, what was going on? She had to know. "What are you doing?"

Kalvin turned around with a grey velvet jewelry box resting in his open palm.

Her hands fluttered to her open mouth. It

wasn't just any jewelry box. It was a Hands Jewelers box. Her heart beat widely in her chest. He would only go to Hands Jewelers for one reason—an engagement ring. No wonder he'd been nervous all night. Laughter bubbled in her chest.

With a shaky smile, Kalvin dropped to one knee. As he opened the box, sunlight glittered off a round brilliant diamond.

She resisted the urge to jump up and down. Tears pooled in her eyes, but she blinked them away and looked up from the diamond to Kalvin.

His blue eyes lit with excitement. "Heidi, will you marry me?"

Tears slipped down her cheeks and she didn't bother to wipe them away. "Holy shit. I mean, yes."

Laughing, he stood and slipped the ring on her finger. His gentle touch sent tingles down her spine.

She looped her arms around his neck and pressed her lips against his. He set his hands on her hips, pulling her closer. She could feel the rapid pace of his heart, thumping against her chest.

He planted one more kiss on her mouth and leaned back, pointing to a bench a few feet down the trail. "You know, I was going to propose on that bench, but you just had to stop here."

She gave him a playful shove. “Don’t even get me started. How could you let me change into a T-shirt and shorts?”

He sent her a knowing look. “I wanted to tell you not to change, but if I had, you would’ve asked me why.”

“That’s true.”

Lifting his hand, Kalvin tucked a loose strand of hair behind her ear. “So, were you surprised?”

Heidi laughed. “Oh yeah.” What an understatement. After worrying that something was bothering Kalvin, his proposal was definitely unexpected. This night had turned out way better than she ever could’ve imagined. Finally letting her excitement get the best of her, she jumped up and down. She was going to be Mrs. Kalafut. Kalvin’s wife. Forever. No more waiting for happily ever after.

As she jumped, movement near the creek caught her attention. Ripples spread across the water near a rock. One frog sat on the rock and two big eyes popped out of the water. The frog on the rock extended its legs, lunging into the water beside the other frog.

Heidi smiled. A frog showed up just when she found her prince charming.

Forever Loved

THE WAX PAPER CRINKLED AS Liv Ryan pushed her elbows into the exam table and leaned forward. Glancing between her bent legs, she craned her neck to see above the mound protruding from her belly. "Am I dilated yet?"

Doctor Yoder straightened from her hunched position and rolled the chair to the side of Liv's bed. "You're dilated to a three and mostly effaced."

Liv's shoulders slumped. Still a three. Not quite fully effaced. No sign of contractions. Would her baby ever get here? In less than a week, her little one would be considered full term.

She dropped her elbows, falling back against the inclined exam table. "I think I'd like to schedule an induction."

Doctor Yoder gave her an understanding smile and walked over to the computer on the other side of the small room. Curly blond strands fell across her face as she typed on the keyboard. "I don't mind coming in on a weekend for you, and I'm on call this weekend." She winked. "Let's go ahead with the 14th, your due date."

"Awesome, Kevin will be able to reschedule all of his meetings by then." She ran a hand over her maternity dress, straightening out the wrinkles above her stomach. Asking for an induction brought a mixture of guilt and relief playing tug-of-war inside her conscience. If only she were more patient, but she couldn't imagine being pregnant much longer. Not with a belly the size of a watermelon. She could barely move her lethargic body to get anything done: housework, yoga, speaking events. No matter what she tried to accomplish, she was drained by the end of the day.

Doctor Yoder strode across the room and held out her hand, pulling Liv to a sitting position. "I'll send the nurse in for the non-stress test. See you on Sunday."

"Sounds good."

The door shut with a soft click and Liv scooted off the exam table. She waddled over to the couch, and pulled her cell phone out of her purse. Getting back on the exam table, she scrolled through the list of names in her phone, clicking on Kevin's name. He picked up on the third ring.

"Hey Babe."

"Guess what?"

"Are you in labor?"

"No." She tried to mask the disappointment in her voice. "But I set a date to be induced."

"That's great. I can't wait to meet Lucy or Calvin."

Liv's heart swelled. Kevin loved being a dad. It was obvious when he arrived home from work and Annabelle and Coleton rushed out to his car, jumping in it to mess with every button on the dashboard. Instead of getting annoyed, Kevin just laughed. Or when he spent part of his night wrestling with Coleton and Annabelle on the floor. She couldn't imagine a better father for her children.

Clutching the phone to her ear, she lay back on the exam table. "Will you reschedule all your meetings next week?"

For a moment, Kevin didn't respond. She imagined him sitting in his office, leaning forward in the leather chair, elbows on his desk. He probably had a pen between his thumb and pointer finger, fiddling with the cap.

"Of course," he said.

She breathed a sigh of relief. As the manager at Northwestern Mutual, it was hard to take off work. And yet, he managed to take off when she needed him, putting his family first. "Thanks. I'll talk to you later."

"Bye, babe."

"Bye." Setting the cell phone on the table beside her, Liv bit her lip, conjuring a sliver of determination. One more week left. She could do anything for a week, including growing a baby.

And yet, it still felt like an eternity. She couldn't wait to meet this child, to have another baby take his or her first breath on Earth. Three years ago, Coleton was brought into the world by his precious birth mother and adopted as their firstborn son. Two years ago, Annabelle became their miracle child, carried for nine months on the dot in Liv's womb.

God had gifted her and Kevin with two beautiful children. The rest were in Heaven. All six of them. Four before Coleton and two before Annabelle. Life had turned out much harder than she'd imagined. When they first met, everything had been so fun, so easy. Meeting on the dance floor at

Brooke and Joe's wedding, going to the farmer's market, making breakfast together, falling deeper and deeper in love every time they were together. But after they got married, the ferocious fertility storm had drenched her with doubt and disbelief.

This wasn't supposed to happen. They were supposed to get married and have lots of babies like they'd planned. But God had a better plan. Going through loss after loss brought her and Kevin closer. Kevin knew exactly how to comfort her, just by being there and letting her cry. He prayed with her and loved her, reminding her that not everything in life could be fixed, but that everything would work out.

She glanced down at her belly, touching the big bump tenderly. Kevin was right. Despite the loss and grief overshadowing years during their marriage, they were blessed to be pregnant with another child.

A MILD ACHE TIGHTENED IN Liv's pelvic region. She sucked in a breath and leaned over, pressing her palm against the fridge. Just an hour ago she'd left the doctor's office. During the non-stress test, the nurse had discovered contractions. But Liv hadn't felt anything. Maybe some pressure, but nothing like real contractions. They were probably Braxton Hicks. No reason to get too excited.

She lifted her hand off the fridge and waddled into the living room. Coleton sat crisscross on the carpet, building a tower of blocks and Annabelle hopped onto the couch, jumping up and down on the cushions. Cartoons played on the flat screen, their high-pitched voices singing the alphabet.

Coleton glanced up from his tilting tower of blocks. A light blond strand slid across his forehead, just above his big blue eyes. "Mommy, when are we going to Bethany's house?"

She glanced at the big rustic clock hanging above the flat screen. If she was really in labor, a play-date would kill time and get her mind off the tension in her lower abdomen.

She lowered her gaze, looking at Coleton and Annabelle as she plastered a smile on her face. She didn't want the kids to realize she was in pain. It would only worry them. "Do you want to go now?"

Another ache arrived, clenching her stomach tight. Sucking in a breath, she pressed a hand against her blue jean dress, trying to gauge the pain. She imagined the pain chart at the hospital, the one with the round faces, ranging from the face with the wide smile to the face with tears. She was probably a three out of ten—the face with the slight smile, since the pressure wasn't too hurtful.

She glanced at the clock again, waiting for the next possible contraction to arrive. Within two minutes, the tightening ache took hold of her abdomen and the pressure intensified. Biting her lower lip, she held back a groan. That contraction didn't feel like Braxton Hicks. Maybe they were the real deal, after all. A smile tugged at her lips.

Annabelle slid off the couch and walked over to Liv, her eyebrows creasing together. "Are you okay, Mommy?"

Liv reached for Annabelle's little hand and squeezed it. "Yeah, sweetie. Mommy's all right." She kneeled down next to the coffee table and reached for her cell phone. Pressing Kevin's name, she took deep, steady breathes as she listened to each ring. *Please, answer. Please, answer.*

"What's up?" The deep timbre of his voice calmed the nerves pinging inside her stomach. He always had a way of calming her down, even when he wasn't trying to.

"You might want to …" She paused for a moment as another contraction arrived and she hunched forward, clutching her stomach. "You need to reschedule your meetings for the rest of the day."

"I thought you wanted me to reschedule for next week."

"I did, but …" She sucked in a breath.

"Are you in labor?"

"I think so." Liv squealed into the phone, unable to contain her enthusiasm. This was really happening. They were going to meet their baby.

"I'll be home as soon as I can. I love you."

The click sounded and Kevin was gone. He didn't wait for her response. He didn't need to—he knew how much she loved him. After being married for seven years, their love went way beyond words. Kevin showed her love when he took her out for dinner every Tuesday night, when he made her breakfast in bed, when he laughed and met her gaze, sharing their own private joke.

"Mommy?" Coleton and Annabelle stared at Liv expectantly and her adrenaline started pumping, fueling her into action. Call both grandmas, contact the babysitter, finish packing, grab the video camera. Hopefully, she wouldn't forget anything and yet, who cared? The baby was coming.

LIV EXPELLED A BREATH AND stepped out of Kevin's sedan, excitement bubbling in her chest. All to-do list items had been checked off and completed. They were at the hospital with packed bags. Relatives were on their way. The doula would meet them in an hour. Nothing left to do besides go inside.

Kevin walked around his car, dressed in blue khaki shorts and a gray T-shirt that fit snugly over his broad, sculpted shoulders. Meeting her gaze, he opened the passenger door and reached for her hand, pulling her out gently. When she had both feet on the pavement, he wrapped his arm around her lower back, giving her a soft squeeze. "Ready?"

Nodding, she stepped out of their embrace and clasped her hands together. "Will you pray first?"

His dark brown eyes narrowed with concern. "Are you kidding? I just prayed two minutes ago in the car."

"You did?" She vaguely remembered asking him to pray, but the car ride had been a blur and she couldn't remember what Kevin had said. "Will you pray again, anyway?"

"Of course." A slow grin spread across his face and the cute dimple in his chin appeared.

She pressed her forehead against his and closed her eyes. His warm, minty breath tickled her cheeks. With every word, her shoulders loosened. Kevin always knew just what to say.

When he finished praying, his fingers grazed her chin and he tipped her face up to his as she opened her eyes. "Are you sure you want to check-in already? You're in really good spirits. During Annabelle's labor, you were in a lot of pain at this point."

"I know. This labor has already been so different."

"Do you want to go for a walk?"

As he dropped his hand to her hip, she leaned her head back and looked up. White puffy clouds moved lazily across the bright blue sky. If she checked-in now, she couldn't leave. She'd be stuck inside the stuffy hospital room, just waiting to push. "That's a good idea. Let's walk around the parking lot. My contractions are still over two minutes apart … but I don't want to go too far."

He wrapped his arm around her lower back as

she took a few cautious steps and leaned into him. She was so blessed to have this amazing man stand by her side. She loved so much about him—his charming demeanor, the way he made anyone feel special, his ability to stay calm under pressure, his easy smile.

Taking another step in the parking lot, her stomach let out a loud, rumbling growl.

Kevin chuckled. He had the kind of infectious laugh that made her lighter and happier, even when she was in pain. "Was that your stomach?"

She nodded. "I forgot to eat lunch."

"Do you want to go inside the hospital and get something to eat?"

She scrunched her nose. Hospital food did not sound good at all. Not on a warm spring day. What really sounded good was ice cream. She looked at Kevin, giving him an innocent look—one that he couldn't resist. "Can we go to Whitey's?"

He shook his head in mock frustration, the dimple in his chin growing deeper. "Of course."

A half hour later, Kevin pulled back into the parking lot and Liv dipped her spoon in the almost empty cup of a cookie dough shake. "Maybe if we have a boy, we could name him Chipper."

Kevin met her gaze and admiration shone in his eyes. "You're unbelievable. How can you be in labor and still be making jokes?"

"I can't help it. I'm so excited." She didn't have room for any other emotion. Not after countless exams and ultrasounds, most confirming her greatest fear—the loss of another baby. No matter how many times it happened, nothing ever prepared her. She loved each and every one of her children, yearning to meet them, to hold them, to guide them through life. She didn't want to let them go. Not so soon. Not ever.

Kevin leaned over the console and pressed his lips against hers. "Let's check-in."

She reached up and ran her hands through his curly brown hair. "What would I do without you?"

LIV HUNCHED FORWARD IN THE hospital bed as Kevin massaged the tense muscles in her neck, the reality of labor taking hold as firmly as her contractions. They would meet their precious baby today. Was it a boy or girl? What would the baby look like? Would he or she have hair?

The nurse waltzed into the room, dressed in blue scrubs and tennis shoes. As she walked toward the bed, she pulled her dark hair into a messy bun. "Hi, I'm Andrea. I'll be with you throughout labor." She guided Liv's legs into stirrups. "Let's see how dilated you are."

Her heart raced as she waited for the results. It had been almost six hours since her doctor appointment this morning. Surely, she was much more dilated by now.

Kevin's fingers stopped moving, and he rested his hands on her shoulders. His gaze lowered to Andrea. "Is she far?" Hope and desperation raised his voice an octave higher.

Andrea's head popped up between Liv's open legs. "Four centimeters."

Liv's eyes widened, her previous excitement replaced with frustration. A freaking four? How was it possible? She'd done everything right. Prayed. Walked. Tried not to focus on labor.

Andrea tugged at her gloves, making a snapping noise as the latex detached from her fingers. Standing up, she gave Liv a warm smile. "Do you want to be admitted?"

Liv bit her lip to keep from screaming. *Heck yes,*

I want to be admitted. Hello. Contractions. Grandma on her way from Springfield. Fat lady wants to meet her baby. Let's get this show on the road.

Kevin started massaging her neck again, kneading his fingers into her tight muscles. "Yes, we want to be admitted."

When Andrea left, he sat down on the bed next to her. Reaching for her hand, he gently rubbed his thumb against her palm. Her fingers itched to touch his face, but a contraction stopped her from moving and she closed her eyes, wincing.

"It's going to be okay. Just listen to your body and you'll be great. And at the end of all this, we get to meet Lucy or Calvin."

"Hopefully, sooner rather than later," she said between clenched teeth.

TWO HOURS LATER, Andrea came back in the room. "Time for another check."

"Good," Liv said breathlessly.

Standing beside the bed, Kevin brushed back her hair as she clutched her hands around the bedposts. *Please be close to a ten. Please be close to a ten.*

"You're at a four." Andrea's voice fell flat, sounding just as disappointed as Liv felt. "Would you like us to break your water to speed things along?"

She nodded like a bobble head, silently screaming *Yes, yes, yes!*

"Great. I'll get everything ready."

Within minutes, water gushed onto the hospital bed. Immense pain clenched its claws around her stomach and tore through her abdomen. Surely, her insides were being ripped apart. She sucked in a deep breath and exhaled. She should have had her water broken sooner. But holy cow. This pain was … much … much … worse.

Kevin set a cold rag on her warm forehead. "You're doing great."

She opened her mouth to respond but bile burned at the back of her throat. Their doula yanked a barf bag from one of the tables. Opening it, Sara held it beneath Liv's mouth as her stomach emptied all of the ice cream. Liv's nose curled in disgust. Chocolate Chip Cookie Dough wasn't so yummy coming back up.

Sara wiped Liv's mouth with a towel and quickly threw away the bag.

Pain crept in like an invisible anchor dropping onto her pelvic muscles. She turned to her side, letting out a long, low moan. If only making noises would get the baby out faster.

Doctor Yoder stepped inside the room and rubbed her hands together like she was starting a fire. "Time to have a baby."

Liv flopped onto her back as Doctor Yoder hurriedly placed scrubs over her dress clothes and stopped at the foot of the bed. The doctor tilted her head, looking down between Liv's legs. "I bet you're close to ten."

"I better be." Closing her eyes, a loud scream escaped through her lips.

Sitting down on a rolling chair, Doctor Yoder's blond curls disappeared as she checked Liv. "Guess what? You can start pushing now."

Despite the cannons of pain shooting between her legs, Liv's spirits rose. She could push now. She'd made it this far with no medication. She couldn't help feeling proud. Her body was capable of growing a baby for nine months and it was capable of making it through labor. Now, she needed to get the baby out safely.

Kevin bent down, his lips grazing her ear. "Push,

babe."

So she did. She leaned forward and clenched her teeth, pushing as hard as she could. Over and over and over again.

"One more time," Doctor Yoder instructed. "I can see the baby's head."

Taking a deep breath, Liv leaned forward farther, and pushed, pushed, pushed.

The baby's head was out, but no sound to be heard. Liv waited for the next contraction, knowing she had to get her baby out immediately. The contraction started and she took a deep breath. One more groan, one more push, and the baby's squirmy body slipped out. Still no cry.

Liv stopped breathing as panic gripped her insides. "What's going on? Why isn't the baby crying?"

Ignoring the searing pain, she sat up straight, watching in fear as Dr. Yoder quickly un-looped the umbilical cord that surrounded the baby's neck.

Kevin squeezed her hand as they waited to hear their baby's cries.

Finally, a beautiful high-pitched wail filled the room.

Liv collapsed onto the bed, taking a joy-filled

breath as Dr. Yoder carefully turned the baby around to face them.

"It's a boy!" Kevin said.

Tears rolled down her warm cheeks as the nurse laid little Calvin Micah Ryan right on her chest. "I'm so happy." Calvin was slimy, snugly, and absolutely perfect. He had a mass of wet, dark hair covering his small head. Blinking, he opened his lids, exposing two dark blue eyes. He looked up at Liv and his little lips parted. Her heart seemed to expand, making room for the immediate love she felt for her son.

Carefully sitting down on the bed, Kevin kissed her forehead. Pulling back, he kept his face inches away from hers. Meeting her gaze, a grin spread across his glowing face. "Calvin's so lucky to have a mom like you."

Liv could feel his smile mirrored on her lips. She was so in love with Kevin she could hardly think. He was her rock. He believed in her, even when she didn't believe in herself. With his encouragement, he ignited an inner strength that she was determined to keep. For him. For their children. For herself.

She broke the space between them and pressed

her lips against his. No matter what happened in the future, she knew one thing was certain: Kevin would always have her heart.

The Promise

JORDON HOOVER TWISTED THE WEDDING RING on her finger as National Guard soldiers strode past, their heavy boots clunking up the ramp of the CH-47 Chinook. Other wives and children crowded around the long helicopter. Their voices echoed across the far, empty side of the hangar, saying their last good-byes as the men headed to Texas for their last training before deployment.

Swallowing hard, Jordon stepped off the ramp and the hangar's cold cement floor seeped through the thin fabric of her black flats. Zipping her fleece up to her chest, she looked up at Ryan, refusing to move any farther away from him. She couldn't say good-bye. Not yet.

Ryan pressed a container of homemade cookies against his Army Combat uniform. "Thanks."

Jordon smiled. "It's the least I could do."

"I'll hand them out on the flight. They'll be

gone before we land." Slipping a hand inside his uniform, he pulled out a Swiss Army knife. "I have something for you, too." He pressed it into the palm of her hand, his dark brown eyes meeting her gaze. "This can be your reminder of me."

Jordon blinked, cutting off any chance of tears. She had to stay strong for Ryan. If he could willingly fight for the U.S., then she could hold it together for a few more minutes. He was so brave to risk his life serving the country, just like his dad, who had recently retired from the Army after twenty-two years of service.

She glanced down at the knife, clasping it tightly beneath her fingers. "What am I going to do without you?"

"You'll be fine."

She pursed her lips. He was only trying to make her feel better by downplaying the difficulty of being apart, but his automatic response stung. The next few months would be hard. Really hard. Ryan didn't realize how his absence would create a hole in her heart that couldn't be filled. "What if my car breaks down?"

"I already programmed Moellers in your phone."

Her eyes widened. "You did?"

"Yeah. Who knows how much longer your Nitro's gonna last? I wouldn't want you to get stranded on some back road without a wireless connection."

"Thanks." Ryan always took care of her car—making sure she had enough air in her tires, doing routine oil changes and battery checks. Now, she'd have to learn to handle these things on her own. She didn't feel incapable, but it was comforting to know Ryan would be there if she needed him.

She bit her lip, a new doubt emerging. "What if someone breaks into the house?"

"You have Shelby and Sally to protect you."

Jordon rolled her eyes. "I doubt they'd even hear a burglar. And if they did, they'd probably just whimper, instead of barking and waking me up."

Ryan put his hands on her shoulders. "You'll be fine," he repeated. "I'll be back before you know it."

She pressed her shoe against the edge of the ramp. Nothing Ryan said could make this good-bye any easier. The moment he left, she would notice every minute, every second. Her hourglass would no longer stand upright with sand gliding from one end to the other. It would remain slightly tilted, the sand slowly drifting down to the bottom of the bottle.

A few more soldiers ambled up the ramp, taking seats inside the helicopter. Ryan glanced at them before returning his gaze to Jordon. His Adam's apple bobbed up and down as he let go of her shoulders. "I better go."

She glanced up at the dark gray sky. Large, dark clouds loomed overhead. "Are you sure it's safe to travel? It's supposed to storm later."

He gave her a knowing look, clearly seeing through her charade to keep him standing with her as long as possible. "We're trained to fly in bad weather."

Jordon blinked back tears. She needed more time. One more night to cuddle. To tell him how much she loved him. Just in case something happened. Her lips quivered as she pushed the thought away. She couldn't afford to think like that.

Ryan tucked a loose strand of hair behind her ear, and set a hand under her chin, gently tipping her face up to his. "I promise I'll come back."

"Don't make promises you can't keep," she said quietly.

Ryan leaned forward, planting a soft kiss on her lips. "I'll give you a call as soon as I can."

The moment his lips left hers, a lump formed in

her throat. She resisted the urge to pull him back for another kiss. To tell him he couldn't go, couldn't leave her alone. She needed more time with him. Enjoying married life. Renovating the house. Starting a family.

"I love you," she said breathlessly.

His gaze lingered on her as he took a step back. "I love you, too."

A tear slipped down her cheek and she turned around, wiping it away as she headed toward the parking lot. With every step, a string in her heart tugged. She would miss him so much. No more holding hands before they fell asleep. Or cuddling on the couch watching movies. Or cooking dinner for him, especially his favorites, like steak or tatter-tot casserole. Cooking for herself wouldn't be the same.

She looked down at the pavement. One day at a time. She would keep busy at school, putting in extra hours to write lesson plans and grade home-work. That was how she'd get through this year.

Maneuvering through the parking lot, she tried to think positively. At least the first good-bye was over with. The sooner Ryan left, the sooner his deployment would be over and they could be together again.

Approaching her red Nitro, she opened the door and collapsed into her seat. With a shaky hand, she turned the keys in the ignition. The car rumbled to life as she stared straight ahead. The rotor blade of the Chinook appeared above the roof of the hangar, followed by the helicopter's massive green body. It rose higher and higher, and then flew away into the dark gray sky.

She pressed a fist against her mouth, choking back a sob. This would be the hardest year of her life.

She leaned forward, slumping against the steering wheel like a wilting flower. Tears streamed down her face. What horrifying things would he experience in Iraq? Would he come back a different person? Would she be able to function without him?

A loud rumbling sounded overhead. She inched forward, her chest pressing against the steering wheel as she peered out the windshield. The Chinook was coming back. Her eyes widened. Maybe the weather was too bad for flying after all.

The helicopter circled above the hangar, then flew away. Again.

Jordon swallowed the lump in her throat as the

tail rotor disappeared in the distance. Whatever reason the soldiers had for coming back, they didn't need to stay.

She fell back against the car seat, long brown strands falling across her face. She closed her eyes, fresh tears pooling against her eyelids as her heart shattered into pieces.

JORDON LIFTED HER LAPTOP OFF the coffee table, facing the webcam toward the fireplace in the living room. A fire blazed below the mantel, its red and yellow flames illuminating the pictures hanging above it. "What do you think?"

Squinting, Ryan scooted forward in his plastic folding chair. "Is that big picture from our wedding?"

"Yeah. It's the one of us walking down the aisle after our ceremony."

"My favorite."

"I know."

"The photo wall looks great." Ryan adjusted his camo hat, setting the bill lower on his forehead. "I can't wait to come home and see all of the improvements you've made to the house."

She lifted her chin, feeling a surge of pride. In Ryan's absence, she'd learned to do a lot of things around the house. Like landscaping the front yard, replacing the kitchen floor, and putting in a new sidewalk.

She put the laptop back on the coffee table, twisting it toward her and plopped on the couch between Shelby and Sally. Shelby opened her eyes and wagged her black tail before falling back to sleep. Sally lifted her head and rested it against the side of Jordon's leg, her long ears flopping against Jordon's flannel pajama pants.

Jordon scratched behind Sally's ears before setting her elbows above her knees. "It was so nice to have you home for Christmas. I wish we could do it all over again."

"Me too."

A familiar ache draped across her chest like the heavy wool blanket covering the back of the worn, leather couch. She grabbed the blanket and set it over her legs. Spending Christmas with Ryan had been everything she'd wanted and more. Cuddling on the couch, watching *The Christmas Story,* cooking and baking, eating a big meal together.

"It feels like forever since I was home." Ryan wiped a bead of sweat trickling down his forehead, a faraway look appearing in his eyes. "Especially after coming back to this heat. It got up to a hundred degrees today."

Jordon scrunched her nose. "How can you function in weather that hot?"

He shrugged and glanced back at the arid Iraqi desert behind him. "It doesn't bother me that much. There are worse things to worry about."

Silence settled over the room. Beside her, Shelby pressed her nose against Jordon's hand. Jordon pulled the dog closer, keeping her gaze locked on Ryan's image. Had he been shot at again? Had he killed anyone? She opened her mouth to ask, and then shut it. Ryan would tell her if and when he was ready. "What have you been up to?"

The blazing fire illuminated the screen as a brief smile flickered across his face. "I've been making movies with the guys."

"Movies?"

"Yeah." Ryan reached for his water, took a sip, and rested the bottle against his thigh. "Actually, would you send some little toy soldiers? We could use them to star in our movies."

She laughed. Ryan was so creative. Even in the midst of war, he could find ways to have a good time. "I'll send the soldiers as long as you let me see one of your movies."

"You got it." Winking, he tugged at his black T-shirt, airing it out. The moment he let go, the shirt stuck to his chiseled chest. "Is it still snowing there?"

"Yeah. We got ten inches yesterday." Jordon glanced out the window. A large white mound pressed up against the glass, creating a stark contrast to the dark, winter night. If Ryan were here, he would've shoveled it off the porch by now. She sighed and looked back at the computer. "School's been cancelled the last two days."

"I bet your students were happy."

"Oh, for sure. Their poems were due today."

Ryan chuckled. "Will some of them still turn the assignment in late?"

"Yes." Shaking her head, Jordon leaned back against the couch and propped her legs on the coffee table. "I hope our kids will be more responsible than some of my students."

Ryan squeezed the water bottle in his hand, the plastic crackling beneath his grasp. "That might be a long time from now."

"The other night, I had a dream we had a little girl. She was absolutely precious."

His lips formed a straight line before his resolve crumbled and he gave her a reassuring smile. "You'll be a good mom someday."

"Someday?" She couldn't hide the desperation in her voice. "I'd like to start trying soon." Her chest ached as she gazed at the carpet, imagining the rosy-cheeked baby from her dream smiling and cooing as she lay on top of a soft pink baby blanket on the floor.

She couldn't wait to have kids. To stay at home and raise three or four. She could already imagine the kitchen filled with her children's giggles as they tossed flour on the table while they baked cookies. She could hear their playful voices carrying across the large expanse of land in their backyard as they played tag around the chicken coop. It felt so real, so attainable if only Ryan would agree to start trying.

He twisted the bottle in his hands. "It wouldn't be fair to have a baby if … if something happened to me."

"Don't talk like that," she said sharply. "You promised you'd come back."

He clenched his teeth, the set of his jaw tightening. "You should be prepared, just in case."

Jordon bit her bottom lip to keep it from quivering. Nothing could prepare her if Ryan lost his life. He was her best friend. He was supposed to be the father of her children. The person she wanted to build a house with, growing old in it together.

In the dining room, the grandfather clock chimed, signaling midnight. She opened her mouth to say more, to keep him talking, but Ryan shifted in his chair and glanced at his watch. No doubt he needed to go.

She pushed the blanket off her lap and set her feet on the floor. Inching forward, she sat on the edge of the couch as if being closer to the computer would bring her closer to Ryan. "I miss you so much."

His dark brown eyes glistened. "I miss you more than you know."

After saying good-bye, she shut off Skype and drifted up the stairs to the dark, empty bedroom. Getting into bed, she slid under the comforter and turned onto her stomach, facing Ryan's side of the bed. His pillow rested against the headboard, puffy and full from weeks of no use. The sheets remained tucked in, still perfectly in place.

She ran her hand over the cold cotton, her chest tightening. "Good night, Ryan," she whispered.

Instead of the deep timbre of Ryan's voice, only the quiet hum of the heater answered her.

Eight Months Later ...

BRIGHT AUGUST SUNSHINE WARMED Jordon's face through the large airport window. The bottom of her dress glided across her knees as she paced back and forth. Where could Ryan's plane be?

"You're making me nauseous." A familiar dark-haired woman stopped in front of Jordon, dropping her backpack next to a row of seats.

Jordon's mouth fell open. She hadn't seen Lindsey since their Bible study a few summers ago. "What are you doing here?"

Stepping closer, Lindsey hugged Jordon and dropped into an empty seat. "I'm waiting for my plane. It's delayed."

"Flight 1456?"

Lindsey nodded.

"That's Ryan's plane. I've been here for two hours already." She started pacing again, glancing out the window. Sunlight poured down on the empty runway. "I'm going crazy. I've waited months to see him and now I have to wait longer."

"Well, the good news is I can keep you company."

"That's true." Jordon tried to mask the disappointment in her voice. Her friend was just trying to be nice.

Lindsey leaned over and tucked a plane ticket in the outside pocket of her backpack. Straightening, she met Jordon's gaze. "So, are you excited?"

Jordon sat down next to Lindsey, her shoulders sagging. "Not really."

"Why are you pacing if you aren't excited to see Ryan?"

Jordon fingered a loose thread on her teal dress. "I'm just anxious."

"Oh."

"Don't get me wrong. I miss Ryan terribly, but I've gone through so many emotions since he left that I'm not sure I'm capable of feeling much right now. Not until I see him."

"I can't even imagine. It makes my problems seem like nothing."

Crossing her legs, Jordon turned toward Lindsey. "What do you mean?"

Excitement flickered in Lindsey's eyes as she looked down at her lap and retied her sweatshirt, pulling it tighter around her small waist. "I just started dating this guy and I really think he could be the one."

"What's the problem then?"

"I don't know if I can deal with some of his annoying habits." Lindsey ran a hand through her messy hair. "He's a neat freak and he still plays videogames. He even dressed up as Superman and went to Comic-Con last year."

Jordon laughed. "So he's a real-life Sheldon Cooper?"

Lindsey cracked a smile. "Uh-huh. How can I live with someone like that?"

"Trust me, no guy is perfect. But if he is *the one,* then you'll learn how to give him grace." Jordon glanced down at the wedding ring on her finger, memories of moving in with Ryan slowly emerging. How odd to think about that early adjustment period after living away from one another for the last eight months.

But she couldn't deny that living alone had its perks. The kitchen table could be used as a sewing space and no longer looked like a gunsmith's shop. There was less laundry to do. No football games on TV, less Comedy Central and more Hallmark movies.

And yet, she'd trade any of it to have Ryan back home for good.

Lindsey pointed up at one of the screens displaying flight arrivals and delays. "It looks like the plane just landed."

Squealing, Jordon jumped out of her chair and slid her hands down her dress, straightening out potential wrinkles. "It was good to see you, but I have to go."

Without looking back, she dashed to the area near the escalator and tucked strands of short, curly hair behind her ear. What would Ryan think of her dress? Would he like her new haircut?

Anticipation traveled through her veins as travelers stepped off the escalator. All around the waiting area loved ones embraced. A teenage boy looped his arm around a middle-age man. A gray-haired couple kissed a little girl with curly pigtails.

More people filled the escalator. No sign of Ryan yet. She checked her phone. No missed calls. No new texts. Where could he be?

She swallowed hard. What if something bad had happened to him?

She glanced up from her phone and drew in a deep breath.

Dressed in his camo uniform, Ryan stepped onto the escalator, his duffle bag draped over his shoulder. His lips parted when he saw her, his dark brown eyes hungrily devouring her face.

She zipped past the other people, weaving in and out of the crowd until she reached the bottom of the escalator.

"Jordon." Her name came out muffled as he lunged off the bottom step, dropped his bag, and scooped her up in a giant hug. She flung her arms around his neck as his strong, muscular arms wrapped around her lower back, breaking all space between them.

Time seemed to stop as she closed her eyes, savoring the feeling of Ryan's body pressed against hers. This was what she'd been waiting for. After all those months of worrying about his safety, she could stay in his arms forever.

And yet, she'd dreamed about this moment for so long, it almost didn't feel real. Opening her eyes, she took a small step back just to make sure.

Keeping her arms around his neck, she drank him in—his sun-kissed tan, five o'clock shadow, and freckles on his nose. She'd missed seeing his face up close and now that he was home, she wanted to memorize every little detail.

Lifting a hand, he softly fingered a curly strand. "I like your hair."

All the blood seemed to rush to her head, and she had to work at getting the words to come out of her mouth. "Thank you."

"Ready to go?"

She gave a reluctant nod. Leaving the airport meant being stuck in the car, sitting in separate seats with the middle console preventing any other touch besides holding hands. If only it were safe to sit next to each other.

Bending over, Ryan grabbed his bag and slung it over his shoulder. As he straightened, he seemed to notice her hesitation, and he reached for her hand, lacing their fingers together before he stepped forward.

She kept a firm grasp on his hand as they walked through the airport out into the warm sunshine and she turned to study his face, mesmerized by how the sun's rays lightened his dark brown eyes to a soft caramel.

Her mind reeled, running through a list of possible things to say. After all this time apart, she had so much to say, but nothing felt right. What would he want her to say? What did he need her to say? Suddenly, it felt like she was walking next to a stranger.

With her free hand, she reached inside her purse, searching for her keys. "Do you want to drive or do you want me to?"

Ryan stopped next to the car and tossed his duffle into the back seat. "Uh, why don't you drive?"

"Okay." She twisted her cars keys around her pointer finger and stepped around him, heading toward the driver's seat. Her shoulder brushed against his, and they exchanged a long, familiar glance before his gaze traveled down to her lips and stayed there, bringing warmth to her chest.

He set his finger under her chin, gently tipping her face up to his. "I can't believe I forgot to do this." His voice sounded hoarse, like it was half-trapped in his throat.

"I was just thinking the same th—"

His mouth cut off her words as he pressed her

flush against his body. Looping her arms around his neck, her heart expanded past her chest and into her ribs, making it difficult to breathe. Their lips melted together and she couldn't tell where her lips stopped and his began.

Not willing to end their kiss, she resisted the urge to smile. Ryan was finally home. Kissing her. Holding her. Just like he'd promised.

Precious Moments

Fall 2015

Mark Halsey turned on the shower, holding his hand beneath the faucet until the stream of water felt warm. He wiped his hand on his stomach, then turned around, meeting his wife's gaze. Rene's big brown eyes stared at him, and for a moment, he got lost in their beauty. After forty years of marriage, she still had that effect on him.

Bending over, he slipped one arm beneath her bare legs and propped the other behind her slender back. As he straightened, he scooped her up against his chest and slowly stepped into the shower. The stream from the showerhead splashed against his back, spitting water against Rene's face. Drops slid off her cheeks down to her neck and onto her chest.

Mark dipped his head, watching the water descend across her porcelain skin before he looked up and gave Rene a mischievous grin. "I think we've taken more showers together in the last few months than we have during our entire marriage."

She gave him a look, one that said, *You would be thinking about that right now.*

He didn't expect anything more from her. Not a playful smack on his cheek. Not a witty retort or a sassy smile. Three years ago, that was exactly how Rene would've reacted. But not anymore. She couldn't speak, stand, smile, or move without someone else's help—she couldn't take care of herself at all. ALS had taken over her body, first corroding her vocal cords and face, then rotting inside her leg muscles, the decay destroying her ability to function on her own.

It was his role to take care of her. To feed, clothe, and bathe her, to move her in and out of her wheelchair, to make her last years comfortable and happy. Looking back at their wedding vows, he'd never imagined how hard it would be to carry out those easily spoken words, *For better or for worse … In sickness and in health … till death do us part.* At nineteen when he'd made that promise, he had felt so optimistic about their future. They would settle down and buy a house, start a family, and grow old together. But their plans hadn't worked out like he'd imagined. When she was fifty-four, Rene started slurring her words and after eight months of doctor visits, she was diagnosed with ALS.

He would never forget those inconceivable words. But he'd be damned if he would let ALS take away Rene without fighting back. He immediately learned everything he could about the disease, discovering that progression was different for everyone and ALS had no cure. He didn't know how much longer they had together, but he was going to make the best of every moment.

Leaning over, his biceps strained as he slowly lowered Rene onto the plastic shower seat. He poured shampoo into his hand, gently massaging the lather through her cute pixie cut. "I talked to Brandon. He's gonna visit next weekend."

Rene tilted her head back and closed her eyes. As he rubbed his fingertips into her scalp, he wondered what else she would want to know about their son's visit. "Brandon didn't talk about any girls, so I don't think he's bringing home a girlfriend. But one of these days, I'm sure he'll surprise us."

Mark rinsed the shampoo out of her hair and ran conditioner through her thin strands. "I was thinking, we should stop by Cory and John's later.

They're decorating the baby's room today."

Rene's lips twitched. If she were able to smile, she would be, and he took her response as a sign to continue.

"Cory already hung up the green curtains you picked out. She said they look really good with the dark oak crib."

The thought of seeing the baby's room made his heart flutter. In just three and a half months, their first grandchild would be here. Baby Dawson had already brought so much happiness back to their family. The little guy gave them something to be excited about, instead of focusing on Rene's illness.

Rinsing out the conditioner, he grabbed a coral colored loofah, lathering her skin until soapy bubbles covered her from neck to toe. He took longer than necessary to wash her completely, but he enjoyed this just as much as she did. In some odd way, helping her with everyday tasks made him feel slightly in control, like he could actually do something to battle this incurable disease that had stolen Rene's body.

Outside the shower, his ringtone filled the bathroom, followed by a vibration against the vanity. He let the song fade out. Whoever it was could wait.

This was his time with Rene.

The ringtone played again, followed by a chime—someone had left a voicemail. He hung the loofah over the shower handle when the phone rang for a third time.

He glanced down at Rene, who was looking up at him. Even with little expression on her face, her thoughts were clear. *We should get out. Whoever is calling has something important to say.* An exasperated sigh escaped past his lips before he reached for towels and dried them off.

He carried Rene to her wheelchair and wrapped a towel around his waist, then grabbed his cell and looked down at the caller I.D. John's name appeared all three times.

Mark's stomach tightened. His son-in-law wouldn't call repeatedly unless something was wrong with Cory or Dawson.

He ran a hand over his mouth, trying to hide his panic from Rene. He didn't want to worry her.

Leaning against the vanity, he clicked on John's name, and held the phone against his ear. His heart beat wildly in his chest. *Please be nothing. Please be nothing. Our family can't handle anything else right now.*

John answered the phone, sounding breathless. "Finally."

"What's up?" Mark kept his tone light, hoping Rene didn't notice the tremble in voice.

"Cory's in labor."

"You can't be serious."

"Her water just broke and we're on the way to the hospital."

Mark rubbed one of his temples. *Holy shit.* If Cory's water had broken, then the baby was coming, ready or not. At five and a half months, Dawson would be premature and underdeveloped. He might be too little to survive.

The blood rushed out of his face. *No, no, no. This was not supposed to happen.* Their grandson was Rene's saving grace. The light in her world of dark despair.

Clutching the phone, Mark took a steadying breath before speaking again. "We'll be there as soon as possible."

Summer 1976

RENE THRAN FOLLOWED DEBBIE PAST a beach

house and stopped in the grass before her shoes touched the sand. Across the beach, a group of teenagers gathered around a stone-encased fire pit. The bright flames lit their shadowed figures and the fading sun reflected off the aluminum cans clasped in several hands.

She bit her lip. Were they drinking pop or beer? She didn't want to get into trouble. If she got a ticket for underage drinking, her parents would kill her. She'd be grounded her entire senior year. One night out with her cousin *so* wasn't worth it. She glanced back at the path, trying to remember how to get to her cousin's lake house from here.

Debbie fluffed her bangs and lowered her tank top, revealing her ample chest. "What's wrong?"

"Are you sure Roy won't care that you're bringing me?"

"Yes. He's super chill and he's bringing a friend with him, too." She opened a tube of lipstick and smeared a bright red color across her lips. Making a smacking noise, she extended the tube to Rene. "Want some?"

She shook her head. "That's all you ever think about—boys, boys, boys."

Debbie slipped the tube into the back pocket of

her jean shorts. "So what?"

"I'm just saying, there's more to life than boys."

"Stop being such a goody two-shoes." Debbie moved her eyebrows up and down. "You need to live a little, starting tonight."

Rene put a hand on her hip. She opened her mouth, then closed it. The practical part of her wanted to remind Debbie of why boys and beer weren't high priorities on her list. But two shirtless guys were making their way across the beach, heading in their direction. Maybe her cousin was right. It was about time she had a little fun.

"Hey girls," said one of the boys. He was short and muscular, while the other boy was slightly taller and wore cutoff jeans that fit snugly over his narrow waist. He had light brown hair sprinkled across his tan chest, all the way down to his chiseled abs. Long, shaggy hair fell across his broad shoulders, swaying as he walked.

Nervous adrenaline pumped through her veins, sending her heart into overdrive. *Holy cow.* He was really cute. She quickly ran a hand through her long brown hair.

The boys stopped in front of them, bringing a sweet, herby aroma along with them. *Had they been smoking pot?* Dread weaseled in beside her nerves, and her stomach twisted in knots. So what if they were cute? She should make an excuse and turn around now. Debbie would understand.

The light haired boy held out his hand to her. "I'm Roy and this is my friend, Mark."

She mumbled hello, barely able to speak as Mark shook hands with Debbie, then her. She let her hand linger in his, enjoying the way his calloused palm felt against her soft skin.

Mark smiled. "You girls want some beer?"

Now would be the perfect time to make an excuse and leave, but with Mark looking right at her, she couldn't think straight. He had such deep green eyes she could get lost in them. Heat formed in her cheeks and before she had a chance to respond, Debbie nodded and looped arms with her, pulling her toward the sandpit.

The boys kept pace beside them, waving at a few people playing sand volleyball a few yards away.

As they grew closer to the bonfire, the sound of voices rose above the crashing waves and a few heads turned in their direction. Debbie dropped her arm and squeezed Rene's hand, whispering, "I think Mark is into you."

"Seriously?"

"Yeah. So have fun and let loose for once, okay?"

"All right." Rene tucked a strand of hair behind her ear. She didn't need Debbie to remind her that she was *so* out of her element.

Mark leaned over the cooler, his shorts growing tight around his butt. He turned around, catching her gaze.

She immediately looked away, playing with a loose thread on her jean shorts. Out of the corner of her eye, she saw him smirking, as if he thought it was funny to catch her staring at him. Her hopes rose a little. Maybe her cousin was right and she did have a chance with Mark. He seemed a little rough around the edges, like he didn't have a care in the world, but there was something about him that had her intrigued.

He handed her a beer and she popped the top, taking a sip. She resisted the urge to wrinkle her nose. This wasn't the first time she'd drank alcohol, but beer was an acquired taste, and she didn't drink it often enough to like it.

Mark arched an eyebrow, giving her a kind smile. "We have water and pop, too. Do you want that instead?"

"Um, I'm fine with Bud Light."

"You looked like you were about to spit it out. Let me get you a water." He grabbed a bottle from the cooler and handed it to her.

"Thanks."

"Do you want to sit down?" He pointed to a long log close to the fire where a couple sat on one end, making out. "There's an open spot."

She glanced away from the couple, looking at Debbie. Her cousin was talking to Roy and twirling a strand of hair around her manicured finger. Debbie probably wouldn't even notice she was gone.

She looked back at Mark. "Let's go."

A grin stretched across his handsome face. Taking a step back, he extended his arm, allowing her to pass. "After you."

Rene headed to the log, suddenly growing conscious about how she walked. Should she sway her hips more or less? Should she take bigger or shorter strides? She groaned internally. What was wrong with her? She needed to get a grip.

Expelling a shaky breath, she sat down on the log and waited for Mark to do the same. She pulled her shoulders back and lifted her chin, trying to appear more confident than she felt. "Is this your first time at the cabin?"

"Yeah. Roy's been asking me to come with him all summer, but I haven't had time. I work a lot." She tried not to notice how big his biceps were as he leaned forward, resting his elbows on his knees. "I finally decided to take the weekend off. It's been nice."

"Where do you work?"

"An irrigation company. I put in underground sprinklers."

"So that's why you're so tan, huh?"

"Yeah." He took a swig of his beer, his eyes never leaving hers. "What about you? Do you work anywhere?"

She crossed her legs. "I work at Aetna Insurance."

"Oh. Do you like it?"

"Yeah, I could see myself working in the insurance industry one day. Plus, it pays for my gas."

His eyebrows rose. "You already have a car?"

"Don't look so impressed. It doesn't have a heater or power steering."

"What kind is it?"

"It's a Belvedere."

He shook his head, sending long, shaggy strands

sliding across his shoulders. "I should have known. You're one of *those* girls."

"What do you mean?"

"Rich."

"My parents are well-off, but I wouldn't say we're rich. They've worked really hard to get where they are." She put her hands on her hips. "Do you have a problem with that?"

He chuckled. "You look really cute when you get angry."

Rene gave him a playful shove, surprising even herself. Somehow, she felt comfortable around Mark as if she'd known him for years. "You didn't answer my question."

His expression turned sober as he put his hand on her knee for a brief moment. "I was just giving you crap. But in all seriousness, my family doesn't have a lot of money. That's why I work all the time."

"That's really impressive." She uncrossed her legs and extended them, resting both feet in the sand. "How old are you?"

"Seventeen. How about you?"

"Same." Rene glanced at the glowing fire, watching the flames dance between the pyramid of wood.

One stick fell to the bottom of the pit, scattering sparks into the darkness. As she watched the small pieces descend into the sand, she couldn't help realizing how much she liked Mark even though she barely knew him. He was very different from most of the boys she hung out with at school. He had a good work ethic, and he wasn't afraid to tell the truth. But she still had some concerns.

Looking up from the fire, she met Mark's gaze. "Can I ask you a personal question?"

He shrugged. "Sure."

"Do you smoke pot?" She tucked a strand of hair behind her ear. "I smelled something funky when you and Roy walked up to us. I'm not trying to be nosy, but …"

Mark chuckled. "You're cute when you get nervous, too." He sat up straighter and took another swig of beer. "And yes, we were smoking before you got here."

Silence settled between them. She wasn't sure how to respond. She didn't like that he did drugs, but she wasn't going to judge him for it either. At least he wasn't a pothead who sat around all day, doing nothing.

He turned toward her, bending his leg and setting it above his knee. "I can tell it bothers you."

"To be honest, I'm not sure what to think about it." Rene rested her head on his shoulder. "The only thing I really know right now is that I like you." The moment the words escaped, she clasped a hand over her mouth. Had she really just said that? What was she thinking? Maybe the problem was, she wasn't thinking at all.

He nudged her with his shoulder. "I like you too."

Her chest swelled. Or maybe thinking was overrated. She liked him and he liked her. She didn't need to know anything else right now.

Mark inched forward to look at her, his face inches away from hers. "Do you, I mean …" He ran a hand through his hair. "Can I have your number?"

She giggled. "You're kinda cute when you get nervous."

A boyish grin spread across his face, but as he leaned back, his biceps and chest muscles bulged, and she was reminded just how manly he was.

"You didn't answer my question," he said in a teasing tone.

Rene tapped a finger on her lips, pretending to contemplate her decision. "Oh fine, I guess so."

"Don't be surprised when I call you tomorrow."

She smiled. "I'll be counting on it."

He put a hand on her knee again, this time leaving it on her leg. Her heartbeat picked up speed and she hoped he didn't notice as he leaned in close. "I might not be perfect, but I'm the type of guy you can always count on."

The intensity of his gaze brought heat pooling low into her stomach. She wanted to believe him, and she hoped more than anything that he was right.

But only time would tell.

Fall 1976

MARK WALKED BEHIND RENE AS they weaved through the thick crowd of people, heading closer to the stage. She glanced back at him once, and he smiled at her to let her know he would keep following. Bright lights illuminated a dark backdrop with *Peter Frampton* scrolled across it in large capital letters. Excited voices from the crowd rose above a Lynyrd Skynyrd song as they waited for Peter Frampton to make an entrance with his band.

This concert would be epic. They were about to hear one of the best rock bands of all times. Adrenaline pumped through his veins. Not just because of the concert, but because of Rene. With her walking in front of him, all he could do was stare at her figure. Tonight she wore white shorts that accentuated her cute butt and legs, and she wore a loose fitting T-shirt that hung low over one shoulder and grew tight around her lean torso. She looked so adorable and sexy at the same time. He couldn't get enough of her.

Turning her head, Rene pointed to two empty seats in the middle of a row. "I think those are ours."

"Sweet. We have a great view." His gaze traveled down to her waist again, lingering for a moment before he looked up. He gave her a teasing grin. "I'm a lucky man. I've already got a great view."

Rene turned around completely, giving him a playful slap on his arm. "You're impossible, you know that?"

"You like it."

"You wish." She flipped her hair over her shoulder and weaved through the crowd to get to their seats.

He followed behind her, still smiling. Over the last three months, Rene had become a little sassier. She was still the sweetest girl he'd ever met, but now she held her own. She'd become accustomed to his humor after spending countless hours on the phone, talking late into the night.

Rene sat down and crossed her legs, her eyes lighting with excitement. "This is going to be so much fun."

"Heck, yeah." He plopped into the seat next to her. Setting his elbow on the armrest, he closed some of the space between them and caught a scent of her flowery perfume. "I'm glad we get to spend more time together."

"I know. It sucks living so far away."

Mark nodded. He couldn't agree more. Rene lived in Millard, Nebraska, thirty minutes away from his parents' house. Technically, it wasn't *that* much of a distance, but with his feelings for her growing, it felt like they were worlds apart. So far they'd only seen each other a handful of times, when he could borrow his mom's car or when she made the trip to see him. It never felt like enough, especially since he'd only taken her out on double dates before tonight. But any time with her was better than none, and he wanted to take it slow. Rene was the real deal, and he wasn't about to mess it up.

He reached for her hand, entwining their fingers. "Next time you visit me, would you like to meet my parents?"

"I would love to." She squeezed his hand. "Family is really important to me."

"I can tell you're close with your parents. I enjoyed meeting them. They're nice people."

She gave him a knowing look. "You're surprised you like them, aren't you?"

"Well ..." He looked up at the brightly lit ceiling as if the right words hung from the beams. "Sometimes upper class people can be a little hoity-toity ..." She opened her mouth to respond, but he continued before she could. "Honestly, I would love to have a family like yours someday. I want to have the type of job where I can provide for my family and not worry about finances."

Rene stared at him for a moment, and he squirmed in his seat. Had he made her upset? That was the last thing he wanted to do.

His eyebrows rose as she leaned over the armrest and softly pressed her lips against his. It wasn't the first time they'd kissed, but it still sent tingles up and down his body. As she looked at him, admiration gleamed in her eyes. "Sometimes, you act wise beyond your years."

Shrugging, he expelled a relieved breath. So he hadn't made her upset after all.

On stage, the lights dimmed and a loud, booming voice filled the stadium. "Ladies and gentleman, please give a warm welcome to Peter Frampton!"

Mark shot out of his seat, pulling Rene up with him. On stage, someone—no doubt Peter himself—strummed his guitar, and blue and red lights turned on, revealing the band. The audience broke into loud applause, shouting and screaming *woot-woots* and *hell-yeahs.*

Joining in, Mark cupped his hands around both sides of his mouth. "You rock!" The blare of Peter Hampton's guitar muffled his words and the band started performing "Baby, I Love Your Way."

He turned toward Rene, playing an air guitar. She laughed, and the sound warmed his heart. He leaned in close to her, singing along with the band. The longer he sang, the more he realized he loved more than just her ways. He loved everything about her.

Fall 2015

RENE'S HEART BEAT SO HARD and fast it felt like it would explode at any minute. Time couldn't move fast enough, knowing Cory was at the hospital in labor. This would be one of the happiest or saddest moments of Cory's life, and Rene needed to be there for her daughter. Even if she couldn't wrap her arms around Cory anymore, her daughter had a way of knowing just how she was feeling. And right now, Cory needed to feel loved.

Mark slapped his palm against the steering wheel and slammed on the brakes. Another red light. "You've got to be kidding me!"

He glanced in her direction and she gave him a look that said, *Anger isn't going to help the situation. You need to calm down.*

The light turned green, and his gaze shot back to the road. He pressed the gas, accelerating way too quickly, and for once, she was happy she couldn't move. Seeing the speedometer would only increase her heart rate.

Directly in front of them, an elderly man's

BMW veered into their lane, then slowed to a snail's pace. Growling, Mark changed lanes and drove past the man, shouting profanities out the open window. Red blotches appeared on his neck, and he clutched the steering wheel so tightly his knuckles turned white.

Rene's hand itched to reach over and grab his hand, but it lay dormant in her lap. Frustration boiled in her veins. If only she could touch Mark or talk to him, to help him calm down.

He slid a CD in the disc player and turned up the knob. Peter Frampton's voice carried through the vehicle. Mouthing the words, his shoulders loosened slightly. No doubt the music reminded him of their concert date.

She'd been thinking about the past a lot lately, remembering those early years, falling in love with Mark. They'd shared so many fun and exciting dates. She still felt the urge to laugh whenever she thought about the time they took Gramma Kitty to *Young Frankenstein,* failing to consider how Mel Brook's humor might not be as funny to a seventy-five-year-old. Her grandma's face had been priceless. Or the time when Mark took her to the dinner theater, and he tried to convince her to eat frog legs.

Or all the weekends they traveled to Chicago for their anniversary. Back then, there was never a dull moment.

Even now that she was sick, Mark left little room for dull moments. He'd helped her achieve most of the items on her bucket list: go ice skating at Brenton Ice Skating Rink; attend a Bears game; go on a family vacation at Honey Creek Resorts; visit Charleston, North Carolina, and Savannah, Georgia; go to a Mumford and Sons concert; attend a Bulls game in Chicago.

And yet, their marriage had dark years, too. Like the time when Mark became addicted to pure cocaine, and he stole from their savings to buy it. The memory of his confession still brought tears to her eyes. Not only because of the hurt and pain he'd caused her, but also because of what he'd said. That he hated himself. All he ever wanted was to be a good husband, father, and employee. After he told her that, he admitted himself into a drug and alcohol treatment center.

She'd considered giving up on their marriage, but Mark was a man of his word. He left treatment a changed person. He spent a lot of time with their family. He took her on dates more often, rekindling their relationship. He started coaching Brandon's baseball team and Cory's soccer team. And when she was diagnosed, he retired to stay home and take of her. She was in love with him more now than ever, and her chest ached at the thought of being separated from him.

The truck swerved, catching her attention, and Mark turned into the hospital parking lot. He beelined for the entrance, slamming on the brakes in front of the sliding glass doors. Running around the pickup, he yanked open the door and grabbed her wheelchair. His eyes looked wild as he met her gaze. "Let's go meet our grandson."

She knew he'd said it for her sake, but a sliver of hope lifted her spirits. *Please be okay, Dawson. Grandma wants to spend time with you before she has to go.*

MARK WHEELED RENE INTO CORY'S ROOM, taking deep, steadying breaths. He had to prepare himself for the worst. If they lost Dawson, he'd need to be the rock for his girls.

Nurses were scattered across the dimly lit room.

Some were standing near the hospital bed with John, who was clutching Cory's hand. Tears streamed down Cory's flushed, red cheeks.

His stomach nosedived, plummeting to the ground. Where was his grandson? He forced his gaze away from Cory, catching sight of an incubator in the corner of the room. A bright light beamed down through the glass, but nurses surrounded it, and he couldn't see. *Was Dawson in there?*

Mark let go of the wheelchair, quickly squeezing Rene's hand as he strode past her and stopped behind the nurses. Holding his breath, he stood on his tiptoes and peered down.

A tiny baby, about the size of his hand, squirmed beneath a nurse's touch as she checked his vitals. His little eyes fluttered open for a moment, then shut again. Faint white hair covered his wrinkly skin.

Mark swallowed hard as he stared at Dawson. His grandson was alive—he had a long way to go before he was in the clear—but he was alive, and that was all that mattered right now. Happiness spread through his chest like helium in a balloon. He resisted the urge to jump up and down, and instead, looked at Cory and grinned. After seeing the baby, he realized she was crying tears of relief.

He turned around to meet Rene's gaze. "Dawson's okay, Grandma."

Rene's eyes twinkled at the sound of her new title.

Later that day, the doctor came back with an update, saying Dawson was too susceptible to infection to be held yet. He would need to stay in the hospital for the next two and a half months, but the good news was Dawson could breathe on his own.

Relief flooded through him. He couldn't wait to hold Dawson, but at least the baby had a good chance to survive.

A MONTH AND A HALF LATER, Mark sat in a chair beside the hospital bed, watching Cory hold Dawson. She pressed her son close to her chest, kissing his forehead. "I love you so much," she said softly.

Dawson made a gurgling noise and Mark chuckled. "He's so precious, honey."

"I know. It feels unreal to finally hold him."

Cory glanced up from her son, and looked at Rene, who sat on the other side of her bed. "I'm so glad you get to spend more time with him, Mom."

Tears slipped down Rene's cheeks. Surely, they were happy tears, but he also knew how difficult this was for her, knowing she'd never be able to see Dawson grow up.

Cory adjusted Dawson in her lap, turning him toward Rene. "Do you want to hold him?"

Knowing the answer, Mark hopped out of his chair and transferred a bundled Dawson from Cory's arms to Rene's. He crouched down beside her wheelchair, propping the baby against her stomach so she could see Dawson's face.

More tears slipped down Rene's cheeks and a beautiful, wide smile stretched across her face.

His eyes widened. It was impossible for Rene to smile. The muscles in her face didn't work anymore. But she was grinning from ear to ear. His heart swelled, bubbling over with elated joy.

Unblinking, he stared at Rene, capturing this special scene as if he had a recorder in his brain. When she was gone, he would replay this moment over and over again, remembering the magnitude of her love.

Made in the USA
Middletown, DE
27 November 2018